Battle Mountain

Clay Parker and his cohorts are what is left of the once infamous Tulley gang. They have waited five years to get the money they stole from a bank, which they believe has been hidden by one of their own – and he has just been released from prison. Now Hugh Donahoe is meeting up with his daughter Mena in the town of Battle Mountain. When his old gang mates confront him, he is killed. The money is not found, however, and the gang suspects that Mena has hidden it in a trunk, which is being carried by Glen Maddox and his mule freighters across the Nevada plains and on its way to Oregon. Parker devises a plan to attack the mule train to get to the stolen money. But Parker is unprepared for the grit of Glen Maddox and his freighters.

Battle Mountain

Matt Cole

A Black Horse Western

ROBERT HALE

© Matt Cole 2018
First published in Great Britain 2018

ISBN 978-0-7198-2668-9

The Crowood Press
The Stable Block
Crowood Lane
Ramsbury
Marlborough
Wiltshire SN8 2HR

www.bhwesterns.com

Robert Hale is an imprint
of The Crowood Press

Typeset by
Derek Doyle & Associates, Shaw Heath
Printed and bound in Great Britain by
CPI Group (UK) Ltd, Croydon, CR0 4YY

Dreams

Mysterious shapes, with wands of joy and pain,
Which seize us unaware in helpless sleep,
And lead us to the houses where we keep
Our secrets hid, well barred by every chain
That we can forge and bind: the crime whose
    stain
Is slowly fading 'neath the tears we weep;
Dead bliss which, dead, can make our pulses
    leap—
Oh, cruelty! To make these live again!
They say that death is sleep, and heaven's rest
Ends earth's short day, as, on the last faint
    gleam
Of sun, our nights shut down, and we are blest.
Let this, then, be of heaven's joy the test,
The proof if heaven be, or only seem,
That we forever choose what we will dream!

Helen Hunt Jackson, 1886

CHAPTER 1

BATTLE MOUNTAIN BOUND

'Deputy Hanrahan looks to have had a bad scare,' commented one of the old-timers on the porch of Pollack's General Store. 'He rides like the devil hisself was chasin' him.'

'Perhaps the Indians are after him,' suggested one old-timer.

Scoffing, the first old-timer replied, 'This area has seen its troubles with the Paiute and Shoshone Indians for sure. But not for some time . . . nah, it has to be somethin' else that has got the deputy in a rush.'

'Well, that is no way to run a good horse,' criticized another of the town's elder citizens. 'Why, in my younger days, no law man would run a lathered horse thataway. Deputy Hanrahan will kill it if he don't damn soon slow the heck down.'

'It don't take much to scare Gus Hanrahan anyways,' lectured the third senior citizen.

'That is a fact,' agreed a fourth older man. 'I swear Gus must have been born nervous.'

The perspiring deputy came racing past the general store, astride his sweating sorrel. He was pudgy, florid and as nervous as a bridegroom at a shotgun wedding – maybe more so, because the trouble in store for the town of Battle Mountain in White Cloud County of Nevada, promised to be somewhat more hectic than any other wedding or ceremony.

Battle Mountain, located in northern Nevada, was midway or thereabout between Winnemucca and Elko. The town was fairly new and the name was often questioned. These old-timers, like most in the town, liked to discuss its origins. The story went something like this: a prospector by the name of George Tannihill discovered rich copper ore and formed a new mining district named the Battle Mountain Mining District. In 1868, the Central Pacific Railroad, the western half of the first transcontinental railroad, built a siding to offload supplies for the mines of the Battle Mountain Mining District. The siding was called the Battle Mountain Switch or Siding. In 1870, the railroad decided to move their station from Argentina to this new area and a town was surveyed out. The town of Battle Mountain was born.

Mr Tannihill reportedly told a newspaper that he

chose the name Battle Mountain because he, Captain Pierson and twenty-three emigrants, fought the Indians here in 1857. There were three attacks near Battle Mountain: one on a single wagon occupied by a man named Wood, the second on a wagon occupied by the Halloway family, and finally an attack on eight men who were part of a government survey crew. The events that occurred that summer near Battle Mountain were well documented in diaries, California newspapers, and the daily records and journals of the men and women who spent the summer near Battle Mountain.

Outside the county law office, which was located half a block uptown from Pollack's establishment, Hanrahan reined up and dismounted. He was delivering an important item of news to the two elderly gents on the office porch – White Cloud County Sheriff Emil Brooks and County Jailer Cecil Albers – and his was one of those nasal, penetrating voices that carries for quite a distance. As a consequence, the news was soon spreading from one end of Main Street to the other.

'The Maddox outfit is comin'!' Hanrahan said speedily.

Sheriff Emil Brooks, a gaunt, watery-eyed and gloomy man, made a grousing sound, bowed his head and clapped both hands to his face. Hatchet-jawed old Cecil Albers jack-knifed out of his chair, hooked his thumbs in his suspenders and thrust his pot belly for Parker – a confident, laborious pose. The aged turnkey always felt seven times more important when the Maddox company visited Battle Mountain. Such visitors habitually developed into wild benders and free-for-all brawls, with Maddox and his half-dozen colleagues eventually incarcerated in the county jail. Albers was not merciless or anti-social; he just happened to enjoy his work, and made quite a ceremony of installing a wrong-doer in a cell. Tonight would be like a bonus. He would really come into his own. Yes, siree.

Seven of 'em!

'I had best get them three rear cells swept out and cleaned out,' Cecil Albers groaned, as he turned and plodded into the office.

'Yeah,' exhaled the sheriff. 'You had best.' He removed his hands from his face, sat up straight and looked his deputy in the eye. 'Gus – now are you absolutely and positively certain?'

Hanrahan had surrendered his mount into the care of a groom from the Double-U Livery Stable, which was situated directly opposite the county jail along Main Street in Battle Mountain. Now, while climbing to the porch, he answered his chief passionately, and still in that nasal, far-reaching whine of his. Locals all along the block stopped, gawked and listened intently.

'Well, damn it all, Emil, don't you suppose I know Maddox's outfit when I see it? I was ridin' home from visitin' my cousin Joseph, out to the Buckeye Creek Ranch. He has been poorly again, has Cousin Joseph. That stomach condition of his. . . .'

9

'Augustus . . . Gus,' said Brooks, clenching his fists on his lanky knees. 'I am real sorry about Justin's bellyache. I will even pay for his next box of bicarbonate – if only you will,' his voice rose higher than Hanrahan's, '*get to the point*!'

'It is Maddox for sure,' a scowling Gus Hanrahan said. 'The whole outfit. All three wagons. I was talkin' the shortcut, ridin' the rim of Painted Point Bluff, when I just happened to glance due south – and there they were.'

'Comin' north by the way of the flats?' asked the older sheriff.

'Same route they always travel.' Hanrahan nodded. 'They were a long ways off, but I guarantee I ain't mistaken. Three big wagons with mule teams. . . .'

'And seven men,' mumbled Sheriff Emil Brooks. 'Seven hoorawin', whiskey-swiggin', rip-snortin' hell-raisers that is old enough to know better.' He raised his eyes skyward and scowled, as though to reprimand all the angels in heaven. 'Why do they have to come rollin' in today? Why does it have to be *this Saturday*?'

'Aw, hell!' groaned Hanrahan. 'I plumb forgot! It is payday for nearly every cowhand in the Battle Mountain area! The town will be crawlin' with cowpokes before sundown!'

'Last time Maddox came to White Cloud County,' Emil Brooks pessimistically recollected, 'him and his hard case crew whupped half the Lazy J outfit.'

'Also, the ramrod of the Stapleton spread,' glowered the deputy.

'Also, Silas Stapleton himself,' sighed Brooks. He shook his head dolefully. 'They named this town wrong, Gus. It sure ain't no Injun place or anything close, especially on paydays. And, with Maddox comin' in, this payday will be the worst yet. Mark my words!' He got to his feet, threw a resentful glance in the general direction of Scossa Flats. 'Well, best we take the usual precautions, not that it will make any difference. Go see if you can recruit a half dozen or so special deputies.'

Ten to fifteen minutes later, a well-dressed stranger, Clay Parker, by name, drawled a question to the ticket clerk of the Battle Mountain railroad depot. He had stopped by to ask if the northbound train would arrive on schedule, and the ticket clerk, runty Zachariah Sprott, had answered in the affirmative. Now, Parker saw reason for a second question.

'What is the big excitement all of a sudden? I get the feeling this town is expecting trouble.' Parker had a dumbfounded look on his face.

The depot office was located on the west side of the railroad tracks and almost directly opposite the triple-storey Commercial Hotel, with the broad and dusty width of South Main Street in between. The Commercial, one of the town's better boarding establishments, catered mainly to transients off the north and southbound expresses of the Galveston and Buffalo Bayou Railroad. Parker and several other men had checked in late yesterday; they occupied adjoining rooms.

He lounged in the outer doorway of the depot

11

office, glaring up Main Street and drawing Sprott's attention to the obvious change in the demeanor of the locals. A short time before, the atmosphere had seemed pretty much as should be expected in a size-able frontier community, a county seat, at 2:30 on a Saturday afternoon. A few stores still open; the majority closed. Locals moving along the boardwalks, pausing to trade small talk with friends. There had been no sense of urgency in the air – until now, when the suspense, the excitement and expectation seemed to affect the entire community, especially the children. The people on the boardwalks no longer dawdled. They jostled about. News of some impor-tance was being carried from house to house. Clay Parker saw several garishly gowned saloon women step into the center of the street, stare attentively towards the south, then hurry back into the honky tonks, saloons, dance halls and gambling houses at which they plied their trade.

Zachariah Sprott filled and lit his bent-stemmed briar and subjected the outsider to an unpremedi-tated scrutiny. He had nothing better to do at the moment. Until the northbound arrived, his time was his own – that was how he saw it. People interested him. He had Parker figured for a traveling salesman – snake oil man or something, maybe more success-ful than the average drummer. What was Parker's line? Fancy stuff, Sprott presumed. High class hab-erdashery, perhaps. He prided himself on his ability to accurately size up a stranger, and just did not realize that his analysis of Clay Parker was extremely wide of the mark.

'You never heard tell of the old mule freight outfit, Maddox and Son?' he asked with a sneer.

'Everybody's heard of Maddox and Son,' Clay Parker replied rather coolly.

'This is the same Maddox,' drawled Sprott, again with a sneer followed by a slight giggle.

'That can't be! That is impossible,' protested Parker. 'By now, old Galen Maddox would be well over a hundred years old.'

'You are forgettin' about the second half of the outfit,' grinned Sprott. 'And 'Son'. Old Galen cashed in his chips a long time back, but young Glen kept the outfit operatin'. Every so often those mule teams haul a couple tons of hard freight into Battle Mountain, and most folks are glad to see Maddox and his crew. A real wild bunch, by golly, but plenty popular.'

'I would have thought Wells Fargo and the railroad would have put the mule freighters out of business by now,' muttered Parker. 'How can they compete with modern transportation? The railroad can deliver in a quarter of the time it takes a mule team.'

'Mr Parker, I have been a railroad man many a long year,' said Zachariah Sprott. 'Before that, I was an expediter for Wells Fargo, so I know what I am talkin' about, when I talk about the transportation business. Plain truth is the railroads don't run everywhere, and neither does Wells Fargo. There are places – far away towns, homesteads, ranches and mining camps – that never see the smoke of a rail-road engine nor the dust of a stagecoach. So how do they get their freight and mail delivered? Why, doggone it, those far away towns would up and die, if it wasn't for the independent operators, the small freight outfits such as Maddox's.'

'All right, I see your point, no need to get all beer and skittles about it,' grunted Parker. 'But, if the son, Glen Maddox, is so almighty popular, how come this town behaves like it is expecting a tornado?'

The station master, Sprott, chuckled softly.

'Those mule skinners,' he explained, 'will be fin-ishin' a long haul there in Battle Mountain. That means they have not seen a big town nor woman cooked meal nor a hot bath in many a long week. They will be rarin' to go – hungry for pleasure – like a passel of trail-herders at a railhead. And it just happens that Maddox and his crew are seven times wilder than any trail-driver, any cowhand, any track layer or miner you ever heard of. Rough? By golly, Mr Parker, they are the roughest you or anyone will ever see.'

'Well, I'm not impressed,' drawled Clay Parker. 'Roughnecks are ten cents a dozen, as far as I am concerned.' He adjusted his hat, began moving away from the doorway. 'You are sure about the arrival time of the northbound train?'

'Just like I told you,' snapped Sprott, 'the north-bound will arrive on schedule.' He glanced up to the sky, paused to sniff, wet the tip of a finger and raised it above his head. 'Storm hits in the meantime, and maybe the rain covers the tracks at Tonopah or Nye basins.'

The visitor ambled back to the Commercial Hotel, followed by Sprott's intent look.

'I am right about him,' Zachariah Sprott assured himself quietly. 'A drummer is what he is. High-class haberdashery, most likely.'

On appearances, Sprott could have been right. Clay Parker's town suit was of expensive material and well-tailored. He moved with the easy assurance of a veteran salesman and, in conversation, was affable, urbane, quick to smile. There was nothing to suggest his true background or the purpose of his visit to Battle Mountain. The local law, as represented by Sheriff Emil Brooks and Deputy Gus Hanrahan, had barely noticed the arrival of Parker and his three associates, because these were men hardened to the necessity of moving clear of lawmen and of protecting their anonymity.

Re-entering the hotel, Parker climbed the stairs to his room on the second floor, a double he shared with the thin, squint-eyed and very nervous Peter Vogel. There was a connecting door, enabling Parker and Vogel to stay in close contact with the occupants of the adjoining room; the tall, hawk-faced Levi Ward and the bushy-browed, heavy-set Frank Humes. These three men were seated by the window, overlooking the railroad depot. From that vantage point, they commanded a view extending far beyond the railroad tracks; they could see almost all the way to the southern horizon. As Parker entered the room,

15

closing the door behind him with a gentle push, they eyed him expectantly.

'Well, how about it?' demanded Ward.

'Everything is on schedule,' announced Parker. He advanced unhurriedly to the window to stand between the chairs occupied by Ward and Humes. 'And all passengers will be accommodated right there at the Commercial Hotel.'

'All passengers,' Levi Ward moved nervously, rubbing his palms together. 'That will include Donahoe.'

'And Donahoe's daughter,' muttered Humes.

'Let's be grateful Donahoe had no son,' shrugged Clay Parker. 'They might have been assigned to a double room and that would have complicated matters.'

'Donahoe's gonna talk,' mumbled Vogel, and he nodded in agitation, as though trying to convince himself. 'He has to talk! We have waited a long time. Five long years. . . .'

'The ticket clerk did not get suspicious?' Ward frowned.

'Why should he?' countered Parker. 'It is quite natural for people to stop by a railroad depot to enquire the times of arrivals or departures.' He moved closer to the window, stared upward. Ward mumbled a query, to which he replied, 'I am looking for storm clouds. That clerk figures himself for a weather prophet.'

'He is plumb crazy,' growled Levi Ward. 'It ain't about to rain.'

'So . . .' breathed Vogel, 'all we have to do is wait.'

'Five years is too long to wait,' scowled Humes. 'When I come face to face with that double crossin' little skunk, I am gonna break every bone in his no-good body.'

'One thing you may rely on, Frank,' drawled Parker. 'Hugh Donahoe will regret the day he ran out on the Tulleys.'

The Tulleys, referred to by Parker, had been Samuel and Abe Tulley, brothers, leaders of the outlaw pack that had plagued the territory along the Nevada-Utah border five years ago. Both brothers had died in the gang's last raid, an attack on a South Nevada bank. A substantial sum – nearly $75,000 in bills of large denomination – had been snatched from the safe of the Sheep Springs Community Bank, after which the nine-strong gang had begun a hectic run eastward towards the Utah line, with a Sheep Springs posse in angry and heated pursuit. During that long chase, both Tulleys had automatically assumed command of the outfit and given the order: 'Every man for himself,' momentarily forgetting that the loot had not yet been divided among the gang, that it was still intact in a grain sack slung to the saddle horn of the horse ridden by Frank Humes. That animal had gone lame and, realizing his capture was only a matter of time, Humes had unhitched the sack and surrendered it to another member of the gang, the genial and somewhat irre-sponsible Hugh Donahoe.

So much for the Sheep Springs raid. It had cost

the lives of the Tulley brothers and the hapless Adolph Flynn, also the apprehension of Frank Humes and Hugh Donahoe. The others, led by Parker, had contrived to elude the posse. Six unscrupulous and vindictive thieves now craved a reckoning with Donahoe who, at the time of this capture, denied any knowledge of the whereabouts of the loot. Clay Parker had not been dismayed; it was exactly what he had expected Donahoe to say to the law.

He had hoped for more definite information, however, when he visited Donahoe in the Fort Shellborne Penitentiary. Both Donahoe and Humes had drawn sentences of five years apiece. Humes had been released some eighteen months ago, his sentence having been shortened for good behavior. Not so the roistering, happy-go-lucky Hugh Donahoe. They had not turned him loose until just a few days ago.

'When I think of the way that coyote back-talked me,' mused Parker, 'I could enjoy slitting his throat.'

'It is just like I told you after they set me free, Clay,' mumbled Peter Vogel. 'He never did aim to divvy up with the rest of us. Keepin' it all for himself, he is.'

'That is what he may think,' leered Humes.

'I stuck my neck out a mile,' muttered Parker, 'growing those whiskers, getting rigged as a preacher to visit him at Fort Shellborne Penitentiary. There might have been some guard recognize me.'

'Well,' grunted Ward, 'he had his chances to play square with us.'

18

'I made him a straight promise,' Parker recalled. 'If he would tell me where he buried the loot, I would save his share for him.' His face clouded over. The nostrils flared and the mouth set in a hard line, the eyes blazed. 'He laughed at me! He said – if I didn't get the hell out of there – he would turn me in to the warden!'

'Clay,' glared Levi Ward, 'do you think there is any chance he spotted Kruse or Gobson?'

He was referring to the fifth and sixth survivors of the Old Tulley gang. This venal half dozen had lived quietly for the past five years, steering clear of the law, subduing their larcenous, murderous instincts and working at a variety of occupations, awaiting the day of Hugh Donahoe's release. They were determined to share in the fruits of the labours of their dead leaders, so they had waited with as much patience as they could muster, counting the days. Nothing had been left to chance. Kruse and Gobson, the two men assigned to shadow Donahoe from the moment of his discharge from the penitentiary, had changed considerably in the past five years. When Donahoe had last known them, they had been heavily bearded and slight of physique. Because they had put on a great deal of weight and were now clean-shaven, Parker thought it unlikely Donahoe would recognize them.

Within the hour of Donahoe's release and his reunion with his sole surviving kin, Parker's spies had dispatched telegraph messages to their four cronies. Parker and daughter had booked passage on the northbound train. Their destination was Stag Ridge, Oregon, and would Clay Parker travel so far from South Nevada without the loot? It did not seem likely to Parker. Somehow, the traitor must have retrieved the cached wealth, unseen by Kruse or Gobson. He was carrying it concealed on his person or in his baggage – of this Parker was convinced. And Battle Mountain, the big town just south of the Nevada—Oregon border, was an overnight stop for all northbound train travelers. From 4:30 p.m. Saturday until 8 a.m. Sunday, passengers and train crew took their ease here and this would be more than enough time for Parker's purpose. Donahoe would be visited and Donahoe would surrender the entire amount of the loot, after some violent persuasion.

'He laughed at me,' Parker sourly repeated. 'Laughed in my face and said I could whistle for my share of the loot. That lousy smart aleck claims we are not entitled to one thin dime because we stayed free and he went to jail.'

'Pretty soon,' promised Humes, 'you will get your chance to pay him off.'

'Just a little while longer,' muttered Peter Vogel. 'Less than two hours from now, we will have him right where we want him.'

CHAPTER 2

THE RECKONING

The seven men known to Battle Mountain as the Maddox outfit were now halfway across Yucca Flats, moving along steadily, not hustling their teams, mind you. At a distance, it could be argued that three heavy-laden wagons hauled by mules were not exactly a sight to fire the blood, to stir the imagination, to warrant welcoming yells, loud hurrahs and much excited laughter from the younger citizens of Battle Mountain. One had to know these seven men, to appreciate the hardships of their trade, if one wished to understand the excitement they triggered while hustling their fractious teams along the main stem of a frontier town.

Glen Maddox had transferred from the driver's seat of the first wagon to the saddle of a high-stepping bay gelding, for the purpose of leading the gang over the last two miles. This was his usual procedure and his prerogative as boss-freighter. The outfit never began a long haul without two saddles packed behind the tailgate of the rear wagon, and two horses tethered to that same tailgate. There were times when it became necessary for a boss-freighter to scout the terrain ahead. For such purposes, a fleet footed saddler was a sight more suited than a squawking Texas bred mule.

'Keep 'em movin', you lazy, good-for-nothin' . . .'

Maddox, riding level with the leaders of the first team, turned in his saddle to bellow abuse and imaginative profanity, not only at the mules but at the men on the drivers' seats of the three rigs. He won a few answering insults in reply, and this was all part of the routine. These mule skinners never took offence, at least not at the scathing remarks aimed at them by fellow freighters. But woe betide the outsider – the town dweller, cowpoke, passing traveler or mine worker – who dared cast such aspersions. The freighters were a clannish sort, tight-knit, welded by a solid bond of loyalty to the name of Maddox and all it stood for.

He was a lot of man, this Glen Maddox, dark-haired, sun-browned, heavy jawed, ruggedly handsome, gregarious in a back-pounding, hand-crushing way. His working rig-out was shabby, but the cartridge belt girding his loins and the Colt .45 in the holster looked to be well cared for. He was grinning broadly, because this had been a long and tiring haul, and it was almost over. In Battle Mountain, they would unload every last ounce of freight, canned goods, feed and grain, and dry goods stashed in these three lumbering wagons that were being pulled across the flats. The teams would be spelled, the men paid off and, for the next several days, the Maddox and Son outfit would relax.

From the seat of the first wagon, he was hailed by two of his closest cohorts, both of whom invited him to study the sky, a sky quickly darkening. The older man, the oldest in the outfit, was Jack Munson, better known as Uncle Jack. He was nudging seventy, a cantankerous little jasper with a white goatee beard. He had been one of the original employees of the company, and Maddox had retained him to serve as cook and relief driver.

'Use your doggone eyes, you blame young fool!' he yelled at Maddox. 'Storm comin' up! You would have noticed before – if you had half the brains that your pappy did!'

'Hey, Mad-dox!' roared the driver of that first rig. 'Ah could swear the old man's right. I do declare that I heard thunder!'

Of the six men in Maddox's employ, none understood the headstrong ways, the strength and weakness, the unpredictable qualities of a freight-hauling mule as sharply as did Jonathan Thomas Quayle, because he had been born and raised in the territory wherein most such freight-critters were bred in, namely the State of Texas. He was known to Maddox, and to the whole outfit, as Texas John. Sinewy, terse and bucktoothed, he was of similar age to the thirty-year-old Glen Maddox, a hard drinker, a determined toiler, a reliable sidekick in the time of emergency.

Maddox raised his eyes to the sky and noted the tell-tale signs. Also, he was suddenly conscious of a change in the atmosphere, one of those changes familiar only to the veteran outdoors man, and a sullen rumbling assailed his acute ears, coming louder than the never-ending clatter of hoofs, the jingle of harness and the creaking of woodwork.

'Damned if you ain't key-rect.' He scowled. And then, rising in the stirrups, he bellowed a command to the other drivers. 'Move 'em up in a hurry! Get them critters runnin' just as fast as they know how! I aim to deliver this cargo to Battle Mountain before the rain turns all this doggone territory to blasted mud!'

'OK by us, Maddox!' yelled the driver of the second rig. 'We don't crave to get slowed down in any damn-blasted mud-trap!' He cracked his whip. 'Heeyaaah! Move – you. . . !'

The third driver cracked this whip, Texas John unleashed a wild yell and, as though lashed by the profanity of their masters, the animals increased their speed. Across the flats, they pounded, urged on by the burly man on the hard-running bay. Maddox led them off the plain and through a rock bordered canyon to the regular trail that led directly into Battle Mountain's main street. Approaching a bend, not one of the three drivers jerked back on their reins; the teams pounded around at speed and the bulky, heavy-laden wooden wagons careened crazily but, thanks to their weight, held to the trail. While they stayed ahead of the coming storm, they could keep to this hectic pace. If the terrain were reduced to a quag-

24

mire by lashing rain, they would be slowed to a crawl.

The first heavy drops were making thudding sounds on the brim of Glen Maddox's Stetson when he sighted the gleaming railroad tracks, the town smoke and scattering of buildings at the southern outskirts of Battle Mountain. The beginning of Main Street was now only a few hundred yards from their wagons.

'There it is!' he yelled. 'Don't nobody let those critters slow down now!'

'Get a movin', you darn Texas mules!' whooped Texas John.

In the past, any time that Maddox's outfit rolled into Battle Mountain, the atmosphere was charged with excitement. This time, it was even more so. There was a touch of rough drama to the spectacle of those three big, wooden, mule driven wagons lumbering into Main Street at such a high rate of speed at the precise moment that the storm struck with all its fury. Thunder boomed and lightning flashed. The rain came pounding down, the first drops hitting the town's boardwalks; men, women, and children waved eagerly at Maddox and his ragtag crew. On they came, the mules struggling through the blinding rain, with Maddox leading them to the very heart of town.

As the cavalcade passed the porch of the law office, Emil Brooks and Gus Hanrahan traded worried frowns. Wistfully, the sheriff studied the six employees of Glen Maddox.

'Same bunch,' he observed. 'Uncle Jack Munson, Texas John. . . .'

'Ellis Allum and Claus Becker on the second rig,' growled Hanrahan.

'And Phil Mitchell and Jacob Maher on the third.' Brooks frowned.

'And the whole hard case outfit led by the worst hard case of all,' groaned Hanrahan. 'Glen Maddox himself.'

'Aw, hell,' sighed Emil Brooks, slapping his knee in frustration. 'This is gonna be one wild Saturday, and that is a fact. It won't take Maddox more than an hour to get those rigs unloaded. And then . . .'

He shuddered. Hanrahan grimaced impatiently and voiced a thought.

'With the railroad deliverin' freight, why are Battle Mountain merchants still payin' Maddox to haul their stock?'

'Loyalty to Maddox's old man, I reckon.' Brooks shrugged. 'You got to admit that, in the old days – before Wells Fargo and the railroad – the storekeepers just had to rely on Galen Maddox. Wasn't any other way of getting stuff delivered from the rail-heads, or from Sacramento or Phoenix or Salt Lake City. And Maddox always delivered on time, gave 'em value for their money.' He shook his head mournfully. 'There will always be storekeepers that will want Maddox to handle their stuff. Which means . . .'

'Which means,' fretted Hanrahan, 'Maddox's gonna be stoppin' by Battle Mountain year after year.'

'And ain't that a frightenin' notion?' The sheriff sighed, at which three stores, a bank, a hotel and four saloons were situated, the three big wagons came to a halt.

Maddox and his men began the formidable chore of unloading, while, from all compass points of Battle Mountain, off duty cowhands came drifting into town to spend their pay on pleasure. Brooks's fears were well-founded; it promised to become a mighty wild Saturday night in the town of Battle Mountain. At around 5 p.m. of that afternoon, the rain had settled to a steady drizzle that made a quagmire of Main Street, and the northbound express train was a quarter hour past due, a fact that caused no surprise at the Battle Mountain depot. It was only to be expected that the train would be slowed down while traveling the mile-long floor of the Yucca Basin. Under these conditions, the tracks might be completely submerged, so delay was inevitable.

On the other hand, the regular routine of the mule freight outfit was proceeding on schedule. All cargo was unloaded in the vacant lot between McCafferty's Hardware and Jepson's Saddler Maker store and, from there, delivered to or collected by the various local merchants to whom it had been consigned. As soon as the big wagons were empty, they were driven uptown and a hundred yards beyond Battle Mountain's northern outskirts, to be quartered at the premises of old Isaac Rickel. This aged horse-dealer-cum-veterinarian had been a friend of Galen Maddox. His barns and corrals were wagons and teams. This was a free service offered to Maddox by old Isaac, but Maddox always showed his appreciation by presenting the horse dealer with a half dozen bottles of a brand of rye available only in San Francisco, plus a box of Havana cigars.

By 5.30, when the northbound train at long last arrived at the Battle Mountain depot, Maddox had collected all freight charges and had paid off his men, who promptly headed for their favorite Battle Mountain saloon, Big Joe's on North Main. They would eat, drink and make merry, not pausing to consider the question of accommodation until much later in the night. By contrast, Maddox and Uncle Jack preferred to get settled into a hotel room, bathe, shave and don their Sunday finest, before sallying forth in search of entertainment. To their favorite local habitat they retired – Pollack's Hotel on Centre Street, a thoroughfare angling off the main stem. There, after an exchange of pleasantries with the somewhat apprehensive management, they took a second floor double, ordered hot baths and, from their pack rolls, broke out their clean shirts and town suits.

During this period in which the boss-freighter and the aged cook were achieving a condition of fine smelling cleanliness and sartorial elegance, the other freighters were 'whoopin' it up' at the saloon owned by Joseph Henry Owens, a pudgy ex-cardsharp known to all and sundry as Big Joe. Texas John was buying whiskey for his friends, for Big Joe's bartenders and percentage girls, for casual acquaintances whose names he could not recall, and for men he had never heard of. Ellis Allum had taken possession of the piano, an instrument at which he performed with much enthusiasm, undismayed by his inability to play any but three well-known tunes. He was accompanied on a borrowed guitar by the tobacco-chewing Claus Becker. Actually, nobody could be certain that Ellis and Claus were both playing the same tune, but nobody cared anyway. Philip Mitchell and Jacob Maher, as was their wont, had bought into a poker game. As usual, the free-spending, back slapping freighters had won all the limelight, and the cowhands were feeling more than a little disgruntled. Cattlemen outnumbered freighters five to one, yet they had to wait their turn to buy whiskey and were being completely ignored by the 'girls' – a loose term used to describe the five or six blousy females of varying dimensions and vintage hired by Big Joe to 'keep the customers happy'.

Prices varied for the ladies depending on their location, age and ethnic background. Why, in San Francisco's Barbary Coast, fees ranged from twenty-five cents for a Mexican woman to a dollar for an American. The regular rate in the cribs occupied by black, Chinese or Japanese girls was fifty cents, while the French women sold their favors for seventy-five cents. Even higher prices than any of these were sometimes obtained by prostitutes of unusual youth and attractiveness and particularly red-haired women. Big Joe did not employ any 'unusual' young girls. The girls were named or at least called Irish Molly, Fatty McDuff, Hambone Jane, Sweet Annie, Lady Pearl, and Wicked Kate.

When Deputy Gus Hanrahan stepped warily into Big Joe's establishment to assess the temper of the clientele, he immediately feared the worst. The cowpokes were becoming increasingly resentful of the attention enjoyed by the freighters and the freighters were cheerfully returning insult for insult.

'It is only a matter of time,' Hanrahan warned his chief, upon returning to the law office. 'There is Bar T hands at Big Joe's tonight, and Pollman men as well. Add them cowpokes to Maddox's hard case crew and what have you got?'

'Trouble most likely,' fretted Emil Brooks. 'And sounds like there could be plenty of it.'

At a quarter to six, when the passengers off the northbound train filed into the lobby of the Commercial Hotel, Frank Humes was seated near the stairs, his face concealed by an open newspaper, his ears cocked to the droning voice of the reception clerk.

'Mr and Mrs Gideon? Yes, ma'am, a nice second floor double. Mr Kersh? Room five, ground floor. Mr and Mrs Donahoe? Beg pardon, folks. Mr and Miss Donahoe. Let's see now. Room seven, ground floor for you, Miss Donahoe. Room thirteen for your father. Yessir, Mr Donahoe, we thank you for the compliment – and we certainly do run a fine house. I am sure your accommodation will be to your liking.'

'Do not worry, son,' Humes heard that familiar drawling voice and nudged one eye around the edge of his newspaper to study the speaker. By gawd! Five years in the big pen must have agreed with Hugh Donahoe's constitution; he looked hale and hearty. 'I am a man of simple tastes.'

'Well,' smiled the clerk, 'I am sure that you will be comfortable in room thirteen.'

And that was all Frank Humes needed to hear, but he remained in the lobby until all the transients had retired to the rooms assigned to them by the clerk. From where he sat, he could see halfway along the ground floor corridor, so he was aware that this would be an inopportune time to pay Donahoe an unsociable visit; Donahoe's daughter was with him.

The ex-convict perched on his bed in his shirt sleeves, puffed at a cigar and grinned amiably at his sole surviving relative. He was mighty proud of the winsome, auburn-haired and comely Mena. She was in her early twenties; she was good-looking and intelligent. Moreover, she had spirit. She was not the kind to let adversity get the better of her. And just as well, considering the hazardous existence she had been forced to live these past five years. She had been almost eighteen at the time of his arrest and trail; he had become a widower some fifteen months before throwing in his lot with the Tulley gang. During his five year prison term, she had worked at a variety of occupations in the settlement of White Pine, which was the town nearest the Fort Shelborne Pen. She had visited him regularly, never chiding him for his irresponsible approach to the demands of parenthood. Loyalty was Mena's strongest point, and he appreciated this more than words could say.

31

She leaned against the closed door, folded her arms over her well-rounded bosom and flashed him a companionable smile.

'Well, Dad? How are you feeling?' she asked.

'Pretty chipper, by gosh,' he grinned, 'considering I have not traveled such a distance in what – five years?'

He was fifty years of age now, a husky, ruddy-complexioned man with iron-grey hair, with a happy-go-lucky disposition and a twinkle in his shrewd brown eyes. She studied him intently, and assured him.

'Things will be better for us from now on. After I marry Antone—'

'I take it mighty kindly that your future husband wants to employ me,' Hugh Donahoe declared.

'Antone knows you would never accept charity,' she smiled in response.

'He also knows I am an ex-convict,' mused Donahoe, rubbing at his clean-shaven chin, 'and that I was once a good-for-nothing thief.'

'A man can change,' she insisted. 'Just look at Antone, he is living proof of *that*. Heaven knows, *he* had to change.'

'From simple cowpoke to lumber merchant,' reflected her father. 'Yeah, that is quite a transformation.'

Mena Donahoe's most recent employer had been the owner of a small restaurant in White Pines. She had waited on tables and, while thus engaged, had met and been courted by a 25-year-old cattleman,

Antone Criley. At the time, her accepting his proposal of marriage, the well-meaning Antone had been just another forty-a-month cowhand, traveling east and west through White Pine with the trail herd outfits running beef from Horton, Arizona to San Bernardino, California. They had no secrets from each other. Antone was well aware of her father's unsavory past, just as she was well aware that Antone's life savings amounted to less than, but almost, $200.

Then came the great chance in Antone Criley's fortunes. A few months before the date set for the release of his future father-in-law, the young cowpoke was advised of the death of a distant relative, an uncle whose name he could barely recall. It transpired that one Justin Alford Criley, a lumber merchant of Elk Ridge in Southern Oregon, had bequeathed all his holdings, every cent of his formidable capital, all his interests in the rich timber belts of the Elk Ridge country, to Mena's husband-to-be.

'It will be hard for me to get used to it,' she confided to her father now. 'I mean, being a wife of a wealthy man. Antone himself feel a mite awkward. . . .'

'That is a terrible ailment for a healthy young buck,' quipped Donahoe. 'Burdened with all that money.'

She chuckled softly, grateful that five years of prison servitude had not robbed her father of his sense of humor.

'Antone's working hard to learn the lumber business,' she murmured, 'and there will be a fine house waiting for us – a good life for you, Dad. He is still a humble man, and he will treat you with respect.'

'Respect.' He heaved a wistful sigh. 'It has been a long time since anybody showed respect for Hugh Donahoe. Excluding yourself, child.'

'That will be enough of that kind of talk,' chided Mena. 'We made a bargain, didn't we?'

'That we did, Mena, my dear.' He nodded. 'That we surely did.'

'No regrets,' she emphasized. 'No more talk of past mistakes. From now on, we Donahoes look to the future.'

'I will go along with that,' he promised, as he got to his feet. 'But, just before we turn our backs on the past – once and for all – there is a little speech I need to make.' He ambled across to her, took her hands in his and eyed her very intensely. 'It is a speech of thanks, Mena, gratitude that a good-for-nothing man like myself could be twice blessed in his lifetime – blessed with a wife of the caliber of your dear mother, Marie, and blessed with a daughter as lovely, caring, and so almighty loyal.' He planted a kiss on her brow. 'I never deserved either of you.'

'I am inclined to agree,' Mena retorted, with mock severity. 'Especially when I think of that awful Widow Begley back in White Pine. You are a terrible heart-breaker, Hugh Donahoe. Why, you visited her as soon as they set you free! Even before you came looking for me, you scoundrel, you had to visit that dreadful Miss Begley. . . .'

'Don't be too hard on Minnie.' He smiled and his

eyes opened wide. 'What I told you of my relationship with Minnie is the gospel truth. I never met a
woman till I went to her store. She is the widow of old
Noah Begley that died last year. Noah and I were cell-
mates. I only called on her to pay my respects, to
assure her Noah's last thoughts were of her.'

'And to have her make that . . .' Mena gestured
helplessly and began giggling, 'that . . . rather
unusual wedding gift.'

Poker-faced, Donahoe asserted, 'I would call it a
right handsome wedding gift.'

'You must be the only father in this entire
country,' she declared, 'who gave his daughter a
corset for a wedding gift.' She blushed, but went
right on giggling. 'A corset – of all things . . . I do
declare!'

'Will you admit,' he challenged, 'that it is a damn
fine corset? I will have you know Minnie went to
great pains to design and sew and—'

'All right – it is beautiful,' she admitted, patting at
her trim waist. 'And a perfect fit.'

'Be off with you now,' her father ordered. 'I know
you are itching to take a bath, and so am I.'

'The gents' bathroom is on the same floor,' she
offered. 'I noticed it as we came along the hall. The
ladies' bathroom is upstairs and I guess I will have to
wait my turn, because every other woman off that
train will have the same notion, I reckon.'

Mena Donahoe pressed her lips to her father's
cheek, opened the door and hustled out. He closed
the door again. The twinkle in his eyes faded almost

immediately; his expression was a serious one, as he returned to the bed. Dark thoughts filled his mind. He was mentally asking a question, over and over.

'Will I live to see her married and settled? Will I see her live a happy life? Will I lead her down the center-aisle of the Elk Ridge chapel, hand her to this Criley boy? He sounds like a damn fine man. Well, thank heaven for that. As for myself . . .'

A few minutes later, it suddenly occurred to him that he should have locked the door, and not just from adherence to the routine of the past five years. He rose up, took two paces towards the door, then abruptly froze. The door had been opened. Quickly, briskly and very quietly, four men entered. The fourth man, the last man to enter, closed the door and stood with his back to the door. A Colt with a cut-down barrel was hefted in his right fist, the muzzle pointed unwaveringly at Donahoe's belly. Donahoe recognized all four of them, including the two weighty jaspers who had travelled from White Pine on the northbound train. Only now, at close quarters, did he realize their identities.

'Well, well, well.' He grinned wryly. 'James Kruse and Carl Gobson. No wonder I did not spot you on the train. Without the whiskers and with all that extra blubber, I would hardly know you.' He looked at the other two. 'Hello, Parker. Hello, Vogel.'

Peter Vogel was the only one not brandishing a revolver. Vogel hefted a .38 caliber Smith & Weston. Thiesen used the hard muzzle of a Colt .45 to prod Donahoe back across the room and into a chair by the window. Kruse maintained his position at the door, while Gobson hustled to the window and lowered the shade.

'You better talk now, Donahoe,' mumbled Vogel, licking his lips 'We got no time to be awastin'- got to handle this quick . . .'

'Poor old Vogel,' chuckled Hugh Donahoe. 'He always was the nervous one, huh, Parker? Never cold-blooded like you and the Tulleys.'

'I would call you a mighty cold-blooded hombre, Donahoe,' scowled Parker. 'It took a lot of nerve to do what you did – to laugh in my face, when I risked my hide to visit you at the big pen!'

'Be thankful,' grinned Donahoe. 'I was tempted – really tempted – to holler for a guard and turn you in.'

Abruptly, Clay Parker turned to growl a query at Carl Gobson, who was carefully examining the carpet bag in the corner nearest the window.

'How about it?' he demanded. 'Is that all, the baggage truck? No valise? Just the carpet bag?'

'That is all of it.' Gobson nodded.

'Yeah,' grunted James Kruse. 'We checked very carefully, Clay. No trunk. No valise. Just the carpet bag.'

'Open it up then,' Parker ordered Gobson. 'And you, Peter, search the room.'

'He ain't had much time to cache it,' opined Kruse.

'We are dealing with one mighty slippery hombre,' countered Parker. 'You already admitted he shook you off his tail a couple of times after they turned him loose. He had his time, James. Time enough to dig up all that money, and—'

'I could save you a heap of time and trouble, Parker,' offered Hugh Donahoe. 'Listen to me for just a minute and you will see how hopeless it is. You think I have it – the loot from the Sheep Springs job. . . .'

'I know you have it!' snarled Clay Parker.

'I should have it,' Donahoe mildly agreed. 'Sure, Parker. I cached it – five years ago – just a little while before that damn posse ran me down.' He tapped at his temple. 'Marked the spot in my brain. I could never forget nor be mistaken. And, right after they discharged me from Fort Shelborne, I went to the place and started digging but it wasn't any use. Somebody found that buried money, maybe a few weeks after I buried it or maybe only a couple weeks gone, so I had to give up on it.' He stared hard at the incensed Parker. 'You have to give up on it, Parker.'

'He is lyin', I bet!' breathed Vogel. 'He always was a tricky one, Clay. You could never trust him.'

He had finished his search of the room. Gobson, who had emptied the carpet bag and felt at every inch of its lining and base, looked at Parker and shook his head.

'Not here, Clay,' Carl Gobson said with a look of disgust on his face.

'The train,' frowned Vogel. 'He cached it on the train. Least, that's my opinion.'

'Not a chance,' grunted Kruse. 'We have kept an

eye on him all the way from White Pine.'

'Donahoe. . .' Parker's voice was soft now, husky, and menacing. 'I will waste no more time on you—'

'Wait,' said Gobson. 'The coat.' He went to the end of the bed to pick up and examine Donahoe's discarded jacket. His questing fingers moved over every inch of the garment, but there were no rustling sounds. 'No. I thought maybe he had it sewed into the lining.'

'Enough of this!' snapped Parker. 'Stand up!'

Hugh Donahoe shrugged, rose from the chair. Gobson ran his hands over him, all the way from shoulders to ankles.

'Nothing doin', Clay,' he muttered. 'And it is a cinch he could not have stashed $75,000 just in his boots.'

'Where is it, Donahoe?' demanded Parker. He swung his left hand in a vicious blow that knocked Donahoe backward over the chair. Donahoe fell heavily, rolled over, began struggling to his feet. 'Last warning, Donahoe! I won't wait!'

'You . . . sure are . . . a hard man to convince . . .' mumbled Donahoe. He was still on his knees, wiping his bloodied mouth on his shirt sleeve. 'It is gone, Parker. You are . . . never gonna see . . . one lousy dollar of that loot. Best make your peace with that and put your mind to that fact.'

'You are a liar!' panted Parker. 'A smug, smart aleck lying son of a—'

'Not so loud, Clay,' cautioned Kruse. 'You will rouse the whole damn hotel.'

'I want the truth!' raged Parker. 'And I want it now!'

'Wastin' . . . your . . . time . . .' groaned Donahoe.

And his voice faded away and he never did regain his feet; he was still kneeling, and Parker, in his blind fury, was striking him again and again, but not with the back of his left hand. His right hand, clutching his six-shooter, rose and fell – rose and fell. Peter Vogel watched in anguished fascination. Gobson and Kruse hurried to Parker and grasped at his arms, but too late. By then, Donahoe was pitching forward on his face, a face bloodied from the terrible head wounds inflicted by the barrel and gunsight of Parker's Colt. He lay limp, making no sound. For any of his old cohorts to have checked for a pulse or heartbeat would have been superfluous. No man could have survived such a savage attack; Donahoe's skull had been crushed.

It was typical of the cold-blooded Clay Parker that he should so swiftly regain control of himself. The color returned to his face. In calm deliberation, he wiped his Colt on a corner of the bedcover, before returning it to his holster.

'The corridor is still clear,' he muttered, 'otherwise Ward would have alerted us.'

'I will take a look out there just in case,' said Kruse.

Callously, Gobson asserted, 'I am glad Donahoe's dead. He definitely had it comin'.'

'But how do we find the money—' began Vogel.

'Shut up, Peter,' growled Clay Parker.

'All clear,' reported Carl Gobson.

'Good.' Parker nodded. 'Let's get out of here.'

Minutes later, they had returned to the room shared by Parker and Vogel. The double rooms at The Commercial weren't all that spacious, and this one seemed overcrowded now. Gobson and Kruse squatted on the one bed, Ward and Humes on the other. Vogel sat by the window, blinking fretfully down into the storm-lashed area between the hotel and the railroad depot. The rain was not intense, but the wind was increasing in velocity. It howled and wailed, while lightning intermittently lit the sky and the thunder rumbled sullenly. Parker paced back and forth, hands behind his back, an unlit cigar working from side to side of his mouth, while he quietly and vehemently gave vent to his feelings.

'That smart-talking coyote – that grinning know it all. . .!'

'Well,' shrugged Frank Humes, 'you sure settled his hash.'

'And that is putting it mildly,' Gobson assured him. 'Donahoe is as dead as he will ever be.'

'Which means,' complained Levi Ward, 'we are just as far from finding the loot as we were before.' He eyed Parker expectantly. 'Clay, maybe Donahoe wasn't lyin'. It stands to reason he didn't have much time for caching the loot. He could not have buried it deep. Somebody else might have dug it up.'

'Isn't that a real possibility, Clay?' drawled Humes, his expression one of true disbelief.

'Anything is possible,' Parker conceded. He stopped pacing, lit his cigar and stared considerately at his associates. 'But I just can't imagine Donahoe taking a chance where that loot was concerned. He was a cool one – cool enough to plant it very carefully, even with a posse hot on his trail. He was the kind of jasper that weighs all the odds, then goes right ahead and makes his decision – and abides by it. I think that is what happened. He planted it. The posse ran him down, and he didn't mind losing five years because, every day of those five years, he was planning how he would live easy for the rest of his life.'

'That money – $75,000,' mumbled Vogel. 'Hell, Clay, it has to be hid somewhere. We know he had time to dig it up and hide it again, when he gave James and Carl the slip. How did he hide it? And would he come so far north and leave it behind, leave it hid somewhere around White Pine? No, by golly. He brought it with him. Bet your life on that.'

Levi Ward paused, then thought to remark, 'Somebody's bound to find the body. There will be tin stars crawlin' all over this hotel inside the hour.'

'What can they do?' challenged Parker. 'Nobody saw us entering or leaving Donahoe's room. The local law will ask a lot of questions and get nowhere. Five years is a long time. We have all changed. Even if our descriptions are on record here, we are still safe.'

'Clay's right,' opined James Kruse. 'We all look a sight different to the old Tulley outfit, huh, boys?'

'Our pockets were heavier when we rode with the Tulleys.' Parker scowled. 'I will make you *hombres* a promise. I will not quit until I have found that Sheep Springs loot.'

CHAPTER 3

SALOON RUCKUS

After a filling meal in the hotel dining room, Glen Maddox and Uncle Jack Munson moseyed along Centre Street to the intersection of Centre and Main streets, looking splendid in their Sunday best, puffing at ten cent cigars and more than ready for a night of merriment. Maddox, in black broadcloth, snow-white shirt and black string tie, looked like an uncommonly cheerful undertaker, or maybe a jovial preacher. Uncle Jack sported a tan derby, a striped shirt minus a collar, checked pants and a Prince Albert coat. The rain had ceased so they had no need of their oilskin rain slickers, which would have cloaked their tailored splendor; instead they were rolled up and tied to their saddles back in the livery. Their boots had cost a month's wages, but they were custom made. The only cowboys who wore ready-made boots were either inexperienced green horns or cowboys saving their money for the custom-made ones.

As they turned onto Main Street, they again noted the serrated flashes of lightning and heard the half-cowed crash of distant thunder, and then Uncle Jack observed, 'We can thank our lucky stars we hit Battle Mountain a jump ahead of that doggone gully washer.'

'I ain't thinkin' of storms or mules nor totin' freight – not tonight, by golly.' Maddox beamed. 'We have swallowed a lot of trail-dust and shed many a pint of sweat these past six weeks, old-timer. What we have earned is a big night at Big Joe's Plenty liquor – plenty purty women – and plenty dancing.'

'If there is gonna be dancin',' replied Uncle Jack, 'ain't no female gonna look at anybody else but me – on account I am the swankiest stepper north of the Rio Grande.'

To illustrate his entertaining and humorous ability, and to the great enjoyment of a passer-by, he broke off to perform a brief but spirited dance right there on the boardwalk, a most involved display of foot tangling which threw him off-balance. But for Maddox's alert and muscular arms, he might have twirled right off the boardwalk and into the muck of Main Street.

'Whoa . . . watch it, pard!' guffawed Maddox, as he deposited Jack back on his feet.

'That was . . . uh . . . just a sample,' panted Uncle Jack, bending over, his hands on his knees.

'Sure, was something.' Maddox grinned. 'And

heaven help the feet of Big Joe's women.'

Eyed askance by the lawman on the opposite boardwalk – the apprehensive Deputy Gus Hanrahan – they proceeded uptown to the swinging doors of Big Joe's establishment. Maddox strode in with Uncle Jack swaggering in his wake and, for a brief moment, the carousing mule skinners abandoned their merry-making to accord him a greeting. From the bar, the gambling tables and the piano, they yelled his name, and laughing dealers and squealing percenters added the weight of their voices.

'Mad-dox!'

That two-syllable word echoed loudly from corner to corner of the crowded barroom, providing a vicarious thrill for the many townsmen who wished they could desert nagging wives and live the exciting life of a mule freighter, and causing many a cowhand to swear in bitter resentment. The cattlemen – representing Bar T, the Pollman Spread, and other ranches – were bunched in the corner nearest the bar, more than a dozen of them, and their indignation was reaching boiling point. A burly brown-haired man of the Pollman spread sourly remarked, 'You would think Maddox was some kind of king.'

'He walks around prancing like a king,' observed a disgruntled employee of the Bar T. 'But what is he? Just a doggone mule skinner with a big mouth and money in his pockets.'

Two giggling percenters – one a buxom redhead, Sweet Annie, and the other a slender brunette, Lady

45

Pearl – jostled each other in their haste to reach Maddox, the readiest spender of them all. He moved on to the long paneled mahogany bar that was polished to a splendid shine, where he put one foot on the gleaming brass foot rail that encircled the bar along the floor. He pushed aside from the ledge a towel that hung so patrons could wipe the beer suds and other liquids from their mustaches. He had toted Sweet Annie piggy-back fashion and Lady Pearl kicking, laughing tucked under his left arm on the way to the bar. One bartender, Ernie, nudged Big Joe McCord, who was lending a hand behind the bar as business was booming, and declared, 'Here we go again, huh, boss?'

'Here we go again, Ernie,' the fat man sadly agreed. He lifted a pudgy hand in greeting, as Glen Maddox lifted the women one by one and perched them on the bar. 'Howdy there, Maddox. Good trip this time?'

Maddox eyed the establishment's owner and nodded. 'Good enough, Joe.'

'You and Uncle Jack drinkin'?' asked Big Joe.

'Did you hear what he said?' Uncle Jack frowned. 'Are me and you drinkin'? Hell?'

'Quit joshin' us, Joe,' chuckled Maddox and he then ordered a drink named after his trade – the Mule Skinner – made with whiskey and blackberry liquor. And if the mood hit him later he would order Cactus Wine – made from a mix of tequila and peyote tea – a drink he learned to favor in Arizona and Mexico. He fished out his wad of cash, peeled off several bills and dropped them on the bar, then raised his voice. 'Everyone, belly up! The drinks are on me, Mad-dox!'

'Mad-dox!' yelled the locals in eager acknowledge, as they surged to the bar and Uncle Jack had to squirm and elbow several men to maintain his place at the bar.

Ernie, the barkeep and his employer, got busy again and the rye, firewater and rotgut flowed fast. Uncle Jack, after his first three drinks, was ready to perform. He captured the buxom redhead, Sweet Annie, and hustled her onto the ten square feet of cleared space respectfully described as the dance floor. Ellis Allum struck up a tune and yelled encouragement. Philip Mitchell put two fingers under his tongue, whistled shrilly, then boomed a warning.

'Uncle Jack is dancin' so everybody watch yourselves!'

'What I crave to see,' lamented Texas John, who was now playing three-card monte, 'is a chance to find the lady . . . I would like to make some money tonight. . . . That money card seems to be hiding from old John tonight . . . maybe I need to switch to poker.'

Claus Becker was playing poker and after he had discarded his borrowed guitar, he said, 'I would like to find a deck with some of them little bitty aces in it or even a few pitcher cards.'

He folded his hand in disgust and saw a violin and bow. He had never had a lesson in his life, and it might be argued that the sounds he produced could

47

never be called music, but he fiddled with great vigor, enjoying himself immensely. Jacob Maher advanced to the dance floor with an eager redhead in tow and the celebrating was resumed with a vengeance.

Again, the barkeep passed a comment to his employer.

'What do you think, boss? Is there gonna be trouble?'

'That is kind of a foolish question, Ernie,' sighed Big Joe McCord. 'The trouble has started already.'

A couple of ranch hands had fragmented from the group of them in the corner and were moving onto the dance floor. One seized Uncle Jack's lady partner; the other slithered an arm about the shoulders of the eager woman who had been on the dance floor with Jacob Maher. The dancing ceased abruptly. Ellis Allum discontinued playing, settled his battle hat more firmly on his dome and rose from the piano stool he had been occupying, with fists bunched and eyes cagy.

'Move away, old man,' one of the cowhands barked at Uncle Jack. 'You are too old for such wild dancin' anyhow.'

And the other cowpokes glared at Jacob and declared, 'You don't own these gals, do you? Haven't bought and paid for 'em, have you?'

'Sonny,' chided Jacob, 'you are talkin' plumb unpolite.'

'Don't call me sonny.' The cowpoke scowled at Jacob.

'You deaf, old man?' challenged the other cowpoke. 'I said to move away from the lady!'

He planted a hand against the old man's flat chest and pushed. Uncle Jack back-stepped off-balance, collided with a chair, righted himself and heatedly raised the war-cry of the mule skinners.

'Mad-dox!'

'Aw, hell,' groaned Big Joe McCord.

And he ducked beneath the bar, not to grasp a shotgun, the traditional discouragement relied upon by all saloon keepers, but to hunt for a pad of paper and a stub of a pencil. Long ago (it might have been after the third or fourth fracas staged by the freighters in this saloon) Big Joe had given up hope of quelling the violence with shouted pleas or by threats from behind the levelled shotgun. The brawlers had ignored him and the fighting had continued, and he had not the heart to discharge two barrels of buckshot at such close range. Nowadays, he was content to assess the damage as it occurred, and collect payment for same in due course.

By the time he rose to his feet, armed with paper and pencil, the battle was beginning. The percentage girls had discreetly retreated to the stairs and those townsmen not desirous of active participants in the impending commotion were edging to the side walls or out onto the front porch. One could enjoy a fine view of the barroom brawl from the front porch of Big Joe's. Especially if the windows were broken, which seemed more than likely.

Ellis Allum had quit the piano stool completely

now. Claus Becker was discarding his fiddle, butting his cigar and rolling up his sleeves. Philip Mitchell and Texas John had lost all interest in the games of chance; they were on their feet, subjecting the local cowhands to a thoughtful scrutiny, as though noticing them for the first time.

'Quite a passel of 'em, huh, Texas?' Philip remarked.

'Well,' shrugged Texas John, 'that never made a difference before now, has it?'

Glen Maddox, grinning in anticipation, was marching across to where Jacob Maher was reprimanding the two aggressive cowhands on the dance floor. To the man who had shoved Uncle Jack, Jacob sternly declared, 'It ain't right and proper to treat an old man in such a fashion.'

'Who are you callin' old?' scowled Uncle Jack, brandishing his clenched fists. 'I am as spry as I ever was, and I can whup twice my weight in grizzly bears – or cowpokes.'

'Don't you preach at us, mule skinner.' One of the other cowpokes who had worked on several spreads scowled at Uncle Jack.

He unwound a wild swing, giving Jacob Maher – the most even-tempered fellow on Maddox's payroll – no option but to strike the first blow in this spectacular hassle. Jacob ducked under that swing and lurched forward, throwing all his weight behind a driving left that slammed into his adversary's belly, knocked all the wind out of him and sent him staggering backward, doubling over, gasping in anguish.

The second cowpoke charged at Jacob, who nimbly sidestepped and thrust out a boot, tripping his would-be attacker.

'He is yours, Maddox,' Jacob called.

And the cowpoke stumbled into Maddox's waiting arms; the hassle had begun. From the corner, grim visaged cowpokes from all the spreads: Bar T, Hannigan, Stapleton and more, surged towards the center of the barroom, with Jacob, Texas John, Claus and Philip stepping up to block their charge. Over the thudding of booted feet, Maddox again sounded the war-cry. Texas John answered with an ear-splitting whoop. The cowhand was tripped by Jacob, then tried to kick Maddox in the groin and, as a reprimand, Maddox lifted him bodily, raised him above his head and hurled him at his advancing colleagues.

That human missile scattered the cowhands, as did the ensuing charge by the freighters. Led by Glen Maddox, they surged across the barroom with fists flailing, and with Uncle Jack Munson yelling encouragement from his safe vantage point; the old cook had hustled upstairs and was viewing the proceedings from the gallery.

Claus ducked to escape a hurled brass spittoon. The spittoon ended its flight in the alley to the right side of the saloon, having hurtled through an open window. Unfortunately, the left side window through which Maddox hurled a cursing Hannigan spread ranch hand had not been opened, and the cowhand disappeared to the accompaniment of a wild yell and a tinkling of shattered glass.

'One broken window,' mumbled Big Joe McCord, carefully noting the damage on his pad. 'One genuine brass spittoon that will likely get stolen by a dealer from the El Dorado Gambling Saloon.'

Surrounding by four hard-fisted cowpokes, Maddox struck out with a will. A fist bruised his cheek and cut his lip but, undaunted, he retaliated. His driving left flattened a nose. His wild uppercut lifted a burly horse-breaker and sent him crashing onto an overturned chair, which promptly smashed beneath his weight.

'One busted chair,' mused Big Joe, still laboriously taking notes. 'Stan Breckinridge will likely charge me three to four dollars to fix it. All right. One chair – let's say four dollars and fifty cents. . . .'

Glen Maddox struck again and again. One of his victims reeled against Texas John. The Texan stamped on his foot and, as he doubled over, brought his knee up to make violent impact with his chin. The cowhand grunted once and dropped to the floor like a poleaxed Texas Longhorn. Maddox's next victim made the serious error of coming back for more. He aimed a hard punch to Maddox's head, missed and, while off balance, was seized and spun around by the hefty boss freighter. Maddox's lashing kick drove him all the way to the batwing doors of Big Joe's and out onto the porch, where he sprawled on face and hands.

'Mad-dox!' yelled Philip Mitchell, who was trading swing for swing with a lean and fast tiring employee of the Zeke Hannigan spread.

'The hell with it, Philip!' chuckled Maddox. 'You don't need any stinking help!'

And that was putting it mildly. Claus and his adversary stood toe to toe. Every time the cowpoke swung, Claus ducked, dodged or parried. Every time Claus swung, he scored. His knuckles were skinned and his arms were aching, but he was not about to desist. At least not until this damn fool cowpoke realized he was licked and had the good sense to fall down.

A brawny cowpoke from another unknown spread leapt at Ellis Allum from behind. He pinned Ellis's arms and clung to his back, as Ellis bent double and stumbled to a corner table. To break the man's grip, Ellis worked his right arm free, raised it and jabbed back over his shoulder with his bunched fist – once, twice, thrice. The third blow was the one that did the job. As he felt the cowpoke weakening, he surged two paces forward, stopped abruptly and heaved. His burden slid off his back and over his head, to collapse onto the tabletop. Simultaneously, Claus Becker administered a short arm jab to another unwary cowhand and, as the man sagged, bent, grabbed his legs, his colleague atop the table and was soon joined by a third. Claus and Ellis jumped to the right and left respectively to avoid being struck by yet another victim of the ham-fisted Maddox. As that third cowpoke sprawled over the table, it gave out a groaning, splintering sound. The legs splayed and cowpokes and tabletop descended to the floor with a loud crash.

'Now add one busted table.' Big Joe was scribbling

again, his stub of a pencil about to break under the pressure he was applying to it. 'That table will cost me . . . ah Lawdy, I'm guessin' five dollars at least. Stan Breckinridge charges heavy. Oh, oh. . .' He noted more damage. 'There goes the felt cover of the poker table. You would think a cowhand would have sense enough to take off his spurs if he has to climb atop a table—'

Hefting a shotgun, squaring his shoulders and arranging his florid face in an expression of unrelenting sternness, Deputy Gus Hanrahan hurried across Main Street and began climbing the steps to the saloon porch. He observed the man sprawled on face and hands just outside the entrance to Big Joe's and was about to finish his climb, when a front window shattered, showering the street and boardwalk in a rain of glass. Like a gigantic and somewhat ungraceful bird, a Hannigan spread ranch hand was hurtling through the smashed window and out onto the porch. He fell with a resounding thud. Thoroughly intimidated, Hanrahan descended the steps and steered a course for the downtown area.

'Too big for just one of us to handle,' he assured himself. 'Better pass the word to Sheriff Brooks.'

He called to his chief as he came bounding along the boardwalk towards the county law office. Sheriff Brooks was just emerging, buttoning his jacket and looking three times as grim as his deputy.

'Up to Big Joe's!' Hanrahan called to him. 'The Maddox outfit again, Emil. Hell, you never saw such a mess!'

'You better handle it!' snapped Brooks, as he came down the steps.

'Uh . . . what. . .?' blinked the stunned deputy.

'I don't mean all by yourself.' Brooks gestured impatiently. 'Get help. Use shotguns and take the usual action. I want Maddox and his hotheads behind bars within the hour. Me – I got to go check on a killin'.'

Deputy Hanrahan stared back at his boss with a blank stare. 'A killin'?'

'Clerk from the Commercial Hotel just brought me the word,' growled Brooks. 'One of the passengers off the northbound train. They found him in his room – his head stove in. I will have to investigate, and that won't please me one little bit. I am no detective, damn it all. This has got my stomach tied in knots.'

For a brief moment, the dutiful deputy stood staring after his chief, who was hustling downtown on the boardwalk towards the railroad depot. Then he turned and trudged back to the heart of town to summon the usual volunteer deputies. By the time he returned to Big Joe's saloon, a half dozen stolid, law-abiding locals were marching resolutely in his wake, all hefting shotguns. They climbed the steps to the saloon porch. They stumbled over the prone brawlers slumbering there and advanced through the saloon's batwings. They moved through the entrance and into the barroom, then came to a halt, gaping incredulously.

'Shamble' was too mild a word. The percentage

girls – Fatty McDuff, Hambone Jane, Wicked Kate, Lady Pearl, Sweet Annie, and Irish Molly – had been obliged to flee all the way up to the gallery, because the ruckus had spilled over onto the staircase. Grinning, cheering townsmen lined the side walls. Unconscious and semi-conscious employees of all the various spreads, ranches, farms, and outfits were sprawled amid the carnage of smashed furniture. Claus Becker, one eye blackened, nose bloody, a concertinaed cigar butt wedged between his teeth, slumped by the bar, was fumbling with bottle and glass, trying to pour himself one last drink, although he was barely capable of remaining upright. Philip Mitchell had been knocked senseless by a hurled spittoon, but probably did not mind, because he was huddled halfway up the stairs, his head cradled in the bare arms of a flabby percenter. Ellis Allum and Jacob Maher were struggling to extricate themselves from the debris over by the faro layout. The only brawlers still in business were Glen Maddox and Texas John Quale. They stood back to back, fists clenched, awaiting further attack.

'C'mon!' roared Maddox, glaring at the horizontal cowpokes. 'Stand up and fight like a man!'

'OK . . . time to break it up!' ordered Deputy Hanrahan.

'You butt out of this, Deputy,' growled Maddox.

'And besides,' grinned a bloody-lipped Texas John, 'we don't hear you.'

Big Joe McCord was still scribbling with his stubby pencil, running a jaundiced eye over the debris and making mental calculations. Two of the befuddled cowhands began the half-hearted effort to regain their feet and resume the conflict. Maddox and Texas John braced themselves, raised their clenched fists warily.

'No more, damn it all, enough!' boomed Hanrahan. 'I said to break it up!'

And to add muscle to his commands, he raised his shotgun. Big Joe yelled a plea; but too late. The shotgun's muzzles were pointed upward when the heavy weapon discharged, and there were to be three casualties – Maddox, Texas John and the saloon's chandelier. This latter, an ornate metal hoop to the rim of which were affixed a dozen small oil lamps, hung from the ceiling by a chain, and that chain wasn't strong enough to withstand the impact of so much buckshot. A couple of links gave way and the chandelier descended towards the barroom floor. Because Maddox and Texas John happened to have been standing directly beneath it, the metal hoop fell cleanly over their heads and shoulders, pinning their arms to their sides. All very neat. All very impressive. Effective, too.

'One chandelier.' Big Joe made a last notation on his list. 'Price seventy-seven dollars and sixty cents – imported special from Carson City.'

'Maddox, you are under arrest!' bellowed Deputy Hanrahan.

'Aw, go jump in the river,' said Texas John, scowling.

CHAPTER 4

BIG NEWS IN TOWN

As Lander County – one of the original nine counties created in 1861 and named for Frederick W. Lander, who engineered the federal wagon route through the area in 1857 – owed its prosperity, for the most part, to the many cattle outfits within its boundaries, it would not have been considered diplomatic for Gus Hanrahan and his volunteers to arrest the fourteen battered ranch hands. Better to arrest the Maddox outfit. Maddox's profits from this last trip would be more than enough to pay Big Joe McCord's damages.

And now, menaced by the levelled shotguns of Hanrahan and company of volunteer deputies, the freighters were surprisingly philosophical. They had satisfied their appetite for food, liquor, dalliance with the opposite sex and a little healthy exercise, the latter being their spectacular set to with the local cattlemen. They did not really mind being taken to jail.

Hell, they could sleep in jail just as easily as under a freight wagon or in some bug-ridden bed in a Battle Mountain doss-house.

Two hours later, when Sheriff Emil Brooks returned to his headquarters, he flopped wearily into the chair behind his desk and scowled at the locked and barred entrance to the cell block. Hanrahan was at the cast iron stove. The stove contained the area for burning wood, while the other was used as an oven. The surface was used as a stovetop, and it even had options for hot and cold water faucets. It was also equipped with a reservoir, which often held a few gallons of water at near boiling throughout the day. But now, it was being used to brew coffee.

'How many of 'em?' the sheriff demanded.

'Same as usual,' grunted the deputy. 'The whole blame Maddox outfit.'

'Which saloon?' asked Brooks.

'Big Joe's,' Hanrahan told him matter of fact-like.

'They are partial to Big Joe's,' mused Brooks. 'Funny.'

'I don't see nothin' funny—' began Gus Hanrahan.

'I was thinkin',' frowned the sheriff, 'of how everybody shows a profit when the Maddox outfit comes to Battle Mountain. The saloon keepers and tinhorns, the women and Stan Breckenridge, the carpenter. Yeah. Specially Breckenridge, because there is always furniture needin' fixin'.'

Hanrahan placed a brimming mug of hot coffee on the desktop, eyed his chief curiously and asked,

'What about that killin' downtown?'

Brooks grimaced in disgust.

'I am stuck,' he complained, 'like a fly in a barrel of molasses. Nobody saw nothin'. Nobody knows nothin'. All I could find out was the name of the decreased. His daughter told me. Seems they were travelin' north together to make a new start in Oregon. He was an old-time bad man name of Hugh Donahoe. Only got turned loose from the Fort Shelborne pen a little while back. He was stony-broke. She is all set to wed up with some Oregon lumber merchant, and was takin' her old man along.'

'One of his old sidekicks caught up with him, I bet,' offered Hanrahan. 'A man could make many an enemy in a pen as big as Fort Shelborne.'

'Or he might have been part of a gang, back when the law put him away,' muttered Brooks. 'Donahoe ... Donahoe... I keep thinkin' I have heard the name before, but I guess I am mistaken.' He leaned back in his chair, took a stiff pull at the coffee and grimaced again. 'I swear I questioned every livin' soul in that damn-blasted hotel – all the northbound drummers, the women, even the kids. Nobody knows nothin'.'

'It could not have been anybody at the hotel, Emil,' asserted Hanrahan. 'A killer don't beat a man to death, then hang around in that very same place and wait for the law to find him. That just would not make sense. What we ought to do is check all the livery stables, find out if any stranger hired a horse in a hurry. Or maybe we could ask around town. Somebody might have spotted a rider movin' out in a hurry.'

'A helluva night for traipsin' all over Battle Mountain, askin' questions,' opined Brooks. 'All that mud. And the thunder and lightning. Would not surprise me if it started rainin' again any minute. Yeah, I sure feel sorry for you, Gus.'

'For me?' Hanrahan frowned.

'Why, sure.' Brooks nodded. 'I just gave you an order . . . or maybe you weren't listenin'. I want every livery stable outskirts of town, you know? Always a chance somebody spotted a rider heading out fast. Any man that rides fast after a rainstorm is just lookin' to break a horse's leg and maybe his own neck or he is a man that feels guilty, you know what I mean?' He gestured to the open doorway. 'Better take a slicker along, Gus. It might rain again any time.'

'Nobody saw nothin', I bet too,' grumbled the deputy, as he reached for his hat and slicker.

'Somebody might have,' countered the sheriff. 'And a description is what we need. There are plenty Battle Mountain folks got sharp eyes and good memories.'

Gus Hanrahan departed and Emil Brooks finished his coffee, lit a cigar and began composing his official report of the murder of Hugh Donahoe – the little he knew of it. The body had been removed from the death scene by a local mortician, Allen Connor and his assistants. The funeral would take place the next afternoon, the attendance was not expected to be big. Throughout its history, there had been very few Sunday funerals in Lander County, but Deacon Andley of the Community Chapel was making an exception. There would be only one mourner, the sheriff expected. In order to attend the service, Miss Donahoe would have to delay her journey to Oregon by one day. There would be another northbound train pausing to refuel at the Battle Mountain depot in the wee small hours of Monday morning, and the local representatives of the Galveston and Buffalo Bayou had promised to arrange passage for Mena.

Thus did Emil Brooks dismiss the Donahoe murder from his thoughts. He had grown old in his job and, in his advanced years, had become somewhat of a cynic and a little lazy – mentally as well as physically. Ten years ago, he would have applied himself to his case with enthusiasm and tenacity. He would have ordered his deputy to the task of an exhaustive check of the law office files. He would personally have studied back copies of the *Territorial Gazette* which were filed at the county records office.

But ten years had changed him. He used little imagination nowadays and, had anybody suggested that the once notorious Tulley gang had held a reunion right here in Battle Mountain, he would have refused to believe it.

One hour later, Connor the undertaker returned to the Commercial Hotel and asked to see Mena Donahoe.

She was seated by the closed window of her room, dry-eyed, garbed in a gown of deep blue, when the night clerk rapped at her door. For five years, she had remained doggedly loyal to her father and, in the passing of those years, had matured from a callow youngster to her optimistic twenties. She was, in many ways, considerably more mature than other women of her age, because life had dealt her many a harsh blow. This latest blow, this wanton slaying of her irresponsible but lovable father, had saddened her to the very core of her being, yet she was beyond hysteria, beyond tears. To weep for Hugh Donahoe would be so futile now – hadn't he always urged her to keep her chin up in hard times?

She glanced towards the door.

'Yes?' she said, her voice barely above a whisper.

'Hello, Miss Donahoe . . . this is the night clerk. A gentleman is here to see you. He apologizes for calling at a time like this, but—'

She cleared her throat. 'Is it the sheriff again?'

'No, ma'am, Mr Connor,' the clerk replied.

'Connor?' Mena asked.

'Yes, ma'am.' The clerk paused. 'The undertaker.'

There was a few moments of silence. 'Oh, of course.' She sighed resignedly, resumed her moody inspection of the windswept area outside the railroad depot. 'I will talk to him now, thank you. The door is unlocked.'

Allen Connor, slight of build and gentle of manner, intruded for only a few minutes. The job of a town undertaker was not easy, and in fact could be rather difficult and even painful at times. As was the case in many towns, Connor was not just the town undertaker, he also was one of its doctors. He was dressed neatly in an all black suit with a white shirt and black tie. Connor politely declined Mena's offer of a seat, stood beside her chair and produced a sealed envelope.

'What is it?' she wearily demanded. 'Your bill in advance?'

'No, Miss Mena.' He frowned. 'I guess you have forgotten. There was enough cash in your father's wallet to cover the funeral expenses.'

She eyed the envelope more intently, observed that it was crumpled and covered with writing – handwriting very familiar to her.

'What. . . ?' she began.

'It was inside his left boot,' Connor quietly explained. 'I thought I should bring it to you right away.'

She took it from him and read the inscription. *To Be Opened Only by My Daughter, Mena Donahoe. And Only in The Event of My Violent Death.*

'I would call those instructions mighty explicit,' offered the mortician. 'Mighty explicit indeed. And I thought the least I could do was bring it along right away.'

'That was very kind of you, Mr Connor,' she acknowledged.

'It was my pleasure,' he assured her, as he bowed slightly then retreated to the door. 'If there is anything I can do, Miss Mena . . .'

'That is very kind of you, Mr Connor, thank you.' She nodded. 'I will remember.'

He left the room, closing the door behind him. After a second perusal of the inscription on the envelope, she tore the flap and extracted a single folded sheet. The message was brief and had undoubtedly been penned by her father but to what purpose? Some strange practical joke?

Mena dear, he had written, *Burn this as soon as you have read it. If you ever do read it, I will be dead – unable to make sure you obey my orders. About that pretty thing I gave you for a wedding gift, take good care of it. Never give it away or let it be burned. Just don't let ANYTHING happen to it. Remember it is the last thing I ever gave you so cherish it always.*

Your proud father.

She heaved a hearty sigh, rose up and walked slowly to the table in the center of the room. There was a heavy brass ashtray with a separate slot containing vestas. She scratched one of the matches to life, held the flame to the envelope and to her father's last enigmatic message, dropped both into the tray and watched them burn to ash, all the time her mind racing with thoughts of what the letter meant. 'What could he mean? A woman's corset is good for only one purpose and I don't need one in any case. At least not just yet. I was only wearing it to humor him, because he darn near begged me to use it. And now – though he is dead and gone – he still begs me to keep it. Why? Am I supposed to feel a sentimental attachment for it, just because it was made

65

by the widow of his old cellmate?' In more ways than one, this was to be a memorable Saturday night in Battle Mountain. The sorrowing Mena Donahoe would have much to remember. So would the locals who had watched and enjoyed that spectacular free for all at Big Joe's. So would Glen Maddox and his salty sidekicks. And so would Milt Milburn.

Mad Milt, Battle Mountain folks referred to him. An uncharitable nickname, and not completely accurate. This aged hunter of quail, deer and jack rabbit was one hundred per cent sane most of the time. His brain became a mite addled and his powers of perception somewhat unreliable after over indulgence in the corn liquor brewed in the still out back of his ramshackle cabin. Heady stuff was Milt's independently produced whiskey. A local bartender with a sound knowledge of all spirituous liquors had once caustically remarked, 'I ain't sayin' Milt's moonshine would harm your insides, but I know for a fact that Dalton Kelley poured some into the tank of his oil lamp and, so help me, that lamp burned bright for one entire week. So you figure it out for yourselves. That liquor is useful enough but not for drinkin'.'

A recluse and a timid soul, Milt Milburn lived all alone in his shack two miles north of town, up by Cosby's Gorge. He trapped a little, hunted a little, fished a little and drank a lot. Tonight, around 10 o'clock, he squatted by the window of his shack, gazing out at the storm. Thunder and lightning made him nervous, except when he was drinking. He was not nervous right now.

At intervals, the lightning lit the sky as brightly as if a large lamp were flashed at the heavens. Milt could clearly see the winding, gleaming ribbon that was the Humboldt River, and that handsome edifice of steel and timber, the railroad bridge spanning the river at Cosby's Gorge. An awe-inspiring sight at this time of night, and under these conditions. That bridge had been designed by the smartest engineers on the Galveston & Buffalo Bayou payroll, and those same engineers had supervised every phase of the bridge's construction. And this was one of Milt Milburn's simple pleasures – sitting by his window at night, swigging his moonshine corn and admiring that masterpiece of engineering.

His mug was half-raised to his mouth when, after a resounding roll of thunder, he saw forked lightning stabbing down from the night's sky, actually striking at the center section of the bridge. There was a blinding flash, a loud, groaning sound as of a hundred souls of torment, then another flash of lightning that momentarily but with infinite clarity illuminated the damage. The bridge had sagged in the middle. It had not collapsed entirely. No. Just that grotesque sagging in the center section and the twisting of the steel tracks, the contortion. Milt's scalp crawled. He squinted suspiciously at his half-empty mug, then set it down on the table slowly and cautiously, as though afraid it might explode.

It took him only a short time to don his hat and rain slicker his old sway-back mare. While engaged in those chores, he mumbled to himself.

'Could have imagined it, I guess. What the heck – no man is perfect. Only one way to make sure. Gotta ride up there and take a gander, get me a closer look. And then if my eyes ain't playin' tricks I had best hightail it to town and raise the alarm. By golly, yes! There are trains that roll over that there bridge on a regular schedule!'

At 10.15 p.m., he was pulling the reins up some forty yards from the south edge of the gorge, and the thunder and lightning triumphed. Every time the lighting illuminated the scene, he won a clear view of the damage. He had not imagined it – no way. That bridge was a goner, and then some.

'Turn around, Betsy,' he ordered the mare. 'Me and you had best head for Battle Mountain and spread the word, pronto!'

Sheriff Emil Brooks did not much appreciate being roused by the county's most infamous moonshiner close to midnight. Battle Mountain was still animated, but at the jailhouse, Maddox and his crew had decided to make the most of their confinement and catch up on their sleep. This section of town was practically quiet, and Brooks liked it that way. He was drowsy on the office couch. At 1 a.m., his deputy would arrive to relieve him. It was considered advisable to man the front office when the jail annex was crowded as on this occasion; no telling what Glen Maddox and his hard cases might try. Cecil Albers, the turnkey, was off duty and confined to his room at the Williams boarding house, sickening for an attack of influenza.

He rolled from the couch, groaned a curse and slogged to the street door, unlocked and opened it. Milt went right on rapping, his knuckles beating an insistent summons on the sheriff's chest. With a grimace of annoyance, Brook brushed his hand aside.

'Milt Milburn – you thimble-brained old reprobate – what the hell do you want at this hour?' The sheriff was unhappy with being woken.

'I noticed,' wheezed Milt, 'there is a train down by the depot.'

'Well, you can't have it, if that is what you're askin',' Brooks bitterly informed him. 'It belongs to the Galveston and Buffalo Bayou Railroad.'

'What I mean,' said Milt, 'is that train better stay right where it is or head back south. It just can't go north.'

The sheriff shot the moonshiner a look of confusion. 'Tell me why not,' challenged Brooks.

'The bridge is down. Just the middle part, mind you, kinda dips now, you know? I saw it happen, Sheriff. . . .' Milt was rambling a bit.

'While you were leanin' on a jug, I reckon,' jeered Brooks.

'It got hit by a bolt of lightning,' asserted Milt. 'Spookiest thing I ever seen, by golly . . . happened so fast. . . .'

'I guess it had to happen sooner or later.' The sheriff sighed.

'You mean that bridge was bound to get hit by lightning?' Milt Milburn said, blinking in surprise.

'No.' Brooks scowled. 'I mean I have always known you would scramble your brains with that wild moonshine you cook up. Been warnin' you for years, haven't I?'

'I seen what I seen!' protested Milt.

'What I ought to do,' opined Brooks, 'is lock you in a cell and let you stew there till you are cold sober.' He crooked a finger. 'Come on, Milt, you crazy old fool. It is for your own good.'

The old moonshiner did not turn and run, when the sheriff moved across the office to take down his keyring from its nail. He just stayed right there on the threshold blinking perplexedly, still mumbling protests.

'How am I gonna make you believe me, Sheriff?' He paused to let the question sit there. 'I was cold sober when I saw it happen!'

'Were you drinkin' your own moonshine?' challenged Emil Brooks.

'Only one tiny snort,' replied Milt.

'That would do it,' decided Brooks. 'Half a mouthful of that rotgut is all it takes. It is a wonder you didn't see something worse, such as the bridge meltin' maybe, or sproutin' wings and flyin' away.' He snapped his fingers, jerked a thumb towards the cell block entrance. 'Let's go, Milt. And no more arguments.'

'As true as my name is Milt Milborne. . .' began Milt.

'Your name is Milt Milburn,' Brooks impatiently reminded him.

'That's what I said,' insisted Milt.

'No,' growled Brooks. 'You said . . . oh, the hell with what you said! I am lockin' you up for the night! Come on!'

He grasped one of the little man's thin arms, made to haul him through the doorway, then paused to squint out into Main Street. Two horsemen had drawn rein at the law office hitch rack and were calling to the sheriff.

'That you in there, Sheriff?'

'This is Brooks,' the sheriff called back. 'Who is that, and what do you want?'

'Cabal and Bedford from the Box J. Got important news for you, Sheriff.' One of the cowhands had a deep resonant voice, so that his every word carried clear to the sheriff inside. 'Bedford and me were on our way home. Lost all our money playin' roulette at the Biltmore Palace—'

'And?' challenged Brooks.

'We took the short cut, rode the south side of Cosby's Gorge. Hell, what a mess! I dunno what happened to that railroad bridge, Sheriff, but I am tellin' you that northbound train better stay clear of it.'

'All bent down in the dead center,' drawled the other cowpoke.

Brooks made a groaning sound, sighed, released his grip on Milt Milburn's arm.

'All right, thanks for ridin' back to tell me,' the sheriff replied.

'We were ridin' on down to the depot,' said Cabal. 'Figured them railroaders better know about it *muy pronto.*'

71

'Yeah, the sooner the better, for sure,' approved Brooks. 'And there are others have to be told. All those northbound passengers at the Commercial Hotel. How about one of you stop by Walton's room and board and rouse my deputy?'

'Be glad to,' Cabal assured him, and the two cowhands rode on.

'You see?' Milt eyed the lawman reproachfully. 'I wasn't lyin' to you, Sheriff, and I didn't imagine it, either. I seen what I seen, like I said.'

'You sure in the hell did that,' muttered Brooks. 'Seems like I owe you an apology, Milt.' He shrugged, forlornly, shook his head and reflected. 'This is some fine Saturday – I don't think. Some fine Saturday indeed.'

CHAPTER 5

ALTERNATIVE TRANSPORTATION

On Sunday, by mid-morning, at which time the mule skinners were released from the county lock-up, all Battle Mountain was abuzz with the big news of the railroad damage. The storm had passed and the day promised to be fine, so many a curious local had harnessed a team to a rig or saddled a horse for the journey out to Cosby's Gorge to inspect the damage to the all-important bridge – all-important insofar as it was largely responsible for Battle Mountain's prominent position on the maps of North Nevada, and for the north and southbound trains of the Galveston and Buffalo Bayou railroad. This railroad was the first to commence operation in this part of Nevada. It was founded by a group of businessmen from San Francisco with the aim of building a rail connection between Nevada, Washington, and parts of Texas. The bridge had been a landmark and the only means of crossing the Humboldt. Until repairs were effected – and this would be a lengthy and involved process – the railroad would have to suspend operations in this area.

Where Glen Maddox and his men were concerned, the sheriff had followed his usual procedure. To have held the mule skinners for trial would have meant several hectic weeks of waiting for the circuit judge and struggling to maintain one's sanity, while playing unwilling host to seven seasoned hell raisers. Brooks had the authority to impose fines and force the payment of damage to Big Joe, who was already negotiating with Stan Breckenridge on the matter of repairs to his premises. Having done so, he issued the ultimatum so oft-repeated as to be downright monotonous. As they filed out into the street, he growled after them, 'I am givin' you exactly twenty-four hours to rest your mules, check your wagons and get the hell out of Battle Mountain. If I catch sight of any one of you this time tomorrow, I will throw you in a cell – and—'

'No, you won't, Emil.' Maddox grinned, pausing in the street doorway to light a cigar. 'You know damn well you won't arrest us again, leastways not this trip. You couldn't stand the strain.'

'And you ain't foolin',' Brooks gloomily assured him.

He tagged Maddox out onto the porch. Because the morning was warm and sunny, Main Street had become somewhat less of a quagmire. Somewhere a church bell clanged and, along the main stem and out of the side streets came the regular church goers of Battle Mountain, the Episcopalians, Baptists, Catholics, and Methodists, on their way to Sunday worship. Uncle Jack Munson, Texan John Quayle and the other mule skinners separated, some to attend services, some to seek an open-house and eat breakfast; the fare provided by the county left much to be desired.

'I don't know what you got to complain about, Emil,' Maddox continued to bait the sheriff, but quietly and without malice. 'You got a real quiet town here. Plumb law abidin'. I reckon you never see enough strife to make you sweat except when us freighters come to town.'

'Think I can take it easy, do you?' challenged Brooks. 'Boy, I got more trouble than I can handle. Passenger off the northbound train got beaten to death in his room at the Commercial Hotel last night while you and your crazy sidekicks were wreckin' Big Joe's saloon. And, as if that ain't trouble enough, the bridge got hit by lightning. It will likely take the railroad a couple months to get it fixed. Meantime, what happens to all those passengers that were headed north?'

'You talkin' about the bridge across the gorge?' Glen Maddox frowned. The sheriff nodded, Maddox emitted a soft, low whistle.

By Judas, the Galveston and Buffalo Bayou, Butterworth, a large, thickset fifty-year-old, was a veteran railroad man, but had never been faced with an emergency quite as worrisome.

He began by confirming the startling news of the railroad bridge having been damaged by lightning.

'It will be quite some time before that bridge can be repaired and reinforced,' he declared, 'so the best we can do is arrange alternative transportation for you folks, and I am sorry to say that won't be any too easy.'

'Mr Butterworth!' A stout, grey-haired matron of similar age to the railroad man rose to voice a complaint. 'I have traveled all the way from North Wendover to be with my daughter in time for the birth of my first grandchild.'

'Well, sure, ma'am.' Butterworth nodded. 'Only natural you would feel distressed about this situation. Don't believe I caught your name.'

'Cross,' said the matron. 'Mrs Myrtle Cross.'

'Ma'am,' said Butterworth, 'we just can't promise to ship you folks any further north for another week. It will take that long to have you escorted east to Fortson's Ford, in rigs by the Galveston and Buffalo Bayou.'

'But that may be too long!' protested the doughty Myrtle Cross. 'My poor daughter . . . waiting for me in Oregon. . . .'

'Plenty of good doctors in Oregon, ma'am,' Butterworth assured her, 'and plenty of good midwives.'

'Why must we be diverted east?' she demanded. 'And what exactly is Fortson's Ford?'

'Fortson's Ford is the nearest safe crossing of the Humboldt after a storm,' explained Butterworth. 'That is a lot of river, ma'am, and running high now, after all that rain.'

Myrtle Cross unleashed a short and bitter burst of dislike against the railroad authorities, the problem of alternative transportation and the unreasonableness of the elements, especially the lightning that had damaged the bridge over Cosby's Gorge. Then, compassionately for all concerned, she resumed her seat and lapsed into a forbidding silence.

Mena Donahoe now put a question.

'Are there no stage lines operating in this area, Mr Butterworth?'

'That is kind of an embarrassing question,' Butterworth replied. 'There was a stagecoach service back before we established the railroad here. They could not compete against the Galveston and Buffalo Bayou. We put them out of business, I am afraid.' He eyed her caringly. 'You are in a hurry to reach Seattle?'

'Stag Ridge, Oregon.' She glared at him. 'I am to be married there.'

'Well,' said the railroad man, 'the Galveston and Buffalo Bayou humbly apologizes, but we could not risk your lives by having those rigs try to ford the river hereabouts. Fortson's Ford is the only safe way. You would be crossing the border inside seven days, and—'

'It seems such a long time,' sighed the thin woman seated near Mena. 'The children were enjoying the journey – their first journey by train.'

'Didn't catch your name, ma'am,' said Butterworth.

'Miss,' she corrected him. 'Not 'ma'am'. Miss Bettie Erickson.''You spoke of children—' he began.

'Eight children,' she nodded, 'aged between six and ten. Five boys. Three girls. They are entrusted to my care until delivery.' Noting the puzzled frowns of her fellow travelers, she hastened to explain. 'I am on the staff of the Holy Cross Orphanage of North Arizona. These children have all been legally adopted by farm folk of the Laurel Valley country, couples unable to have children of their own. It is not a large community, so the children will still have the chance to grow up together. It is a wonderful thing.'

'My fiancé has mentioned Laurel Valley,' offered Mena. 'I understand it is less than twenty miles north of Stag Ridge.'

With upsetting candor, Mrs Cross opined, 'You don't look strong enough to handle eight frisky youngsters.'

'She manages fine,' smiled Mena. 'I offered to lend a hand, after I boarded the train at White Pines, but . . .'

'It was kind of you to want to help, Miss Donahoe,' the gaunt spinster acknowledged. 'And I may have to accept your offer.' She sighed forlornly. 'The journey east to the fording place will be more tiring than the train journey, I fear.'

One of the two affluent looking men seated at the

rear of the dining room called a blunt query.

'Have you considered every other possibility? Is this the only alternative open to us?' a gentleman spoke up, his hat in hand.

'Excuse me, Mr. . .?' said Butterworth.

'Wayne Buford.' The affluent looking man rose to his feet now, indicating the equally well-groomed man in the chair beside his. 'And my brother, Liam.'

Mena briefly studied the brothers Buford, while the depot manager stressed the palpable danger in attempting to ford the great river in the immediate vicinity of Battle Mountain. They were not young men; both looked to be in their mid to late forties, but they were well-preserved, tolerably good-looking and of affable disposition. She recalled that, during her journey up from White Pines with her father, these men had been well-mannered and thoughtful of the beleaguered Miss Erickson and the doughty Mrs Cross.

'I am right sorry, Mr Buford,' said Butterworth, in conclusion, 'if you and your brother have urgent reasons for wanting to move on. I can only repeat that the Galveston and Buffalo Bayou organization deeply regrets this delay, and will arrange your alternative transportation just as quickly as possible.'

'Our reasons,' frowned Wayne Buford, 'aren't as urgent as those stated by these good ladies, Mrs Cross and Miss Bettie. We are on our way to Klamath Falls as a liberal township, but there is no newspaper, and that is how Liam and I got interested in coming north.'

'I noticed your names on the freight list, come to think of it.' Butterworth pondered on this. 'Those large crates in the baggage car are consigned to Klamath Falls in your name. May I ask. . .?'

'It is no secret,' Wayne Buford shrugged and grinned. 'Those crates contain a brand new Imprenta Press V John Sherwin printing press, ready to be assembled when we reach Klamath Falls, also type-cases and other equipment necessary to the running of a newspaper.'

'That is mighty heavy freight,' reflected Butterworth. 'I can arrange transportation for your-selves and your personal baggage, Mr Buford, but the printing press may have to be shipped on the rail, due to its weight.'

'By rail,' mused Wayne Buford. 'In other words, we would have to wait until the bridge has been repaired.' He nodded graciously to the depot manager, resumed his seat and quietly remarked to his brother, 'I have never even seen the Imprenta Press V John Sherwin press but I am homesick for it already. This delay is something I was not counting on.'

'Brother,' grinned Liam Buford, 'a bolt of light-ning is something nobody expected.'

'I guess we have heard all that Butterworth can tell us,' muttered the older brother. 'The morning has become warm, and I could use a glass of beer – tall and cool. Do you suppose we would find a saloon open on Sunday morning in Battle Mountain?'

'Only one way to find that out.' The younger

brother shrugged.

The Bufords got up, politely begged to be excused, then donned their hats and ambled out of the dining room and through the lobby to Main Street.

Sauntering towards the heart of town, the brothers came to a saloon that was open for business, the small hole in the wall establishment presided over by the scrawny and genial Don Fisher. There, they hooked boot heels on the brass rail below the bar, propped elbows on the bar top, quaffed cold beer and discussed their predicament. They were Fisher's only customers at that hour, and he could not help but overhear. Were these gents in the market for a friendly suggestion? They unquestionably were and what could he suggest? Thus, the potential proprietors of a North Oregon newspaper learned something of the almost legendary Maddox outfit, the devil-may-care freighters who had driven their mules over mountains and deserts and across many a river in their day.

'Many a river,' Fisher emphasized, 'that was runnin' higher than the Humboldt. I am tellin' you this Maddox is one tough hombre. There ain't nothin' he is afraid of.'

'There is something I am afraid of, friend.' Wayne Buford frowned. 'The possibility of losing all our equipment, seeing it carried downstream in a wagon overturned by a flood current.' He thought to add, 'But thanks for the suggestion.'

'It wouldn't do any harm to talk it over with this

Maddox fella,' opined Liam Buford.

'Where would we find him?' asked the elder Buford brother.

'Gaskin's place,' Fisher told him. 'The horse dealer. You just travel due north out of town a little ways. Can't miss it.'

A short time later, the brothers Buford were entering a large barn beyond a network of corrals on the Gaskin property, to introduce themselves to the tall, rugged looking man inspecting the forehoof of a skittish mule. They were about to make Maddox a proposition – one that would plunge them headlong into hectic adventure.

CHAPTER 6

ADDING THE PLANKS

Having given Wayne Buford a hearing, Glen Maddox let the brothers out into the bright Nevada sunshine. They climbed to the top rail of a corral housing half a dozen of the freighters' animals and, while his visitors presented him with a fine cigar and lit it for him even, he considered their proposition.

'One rig – to tote you and your gear to Klamath Falls, Oregon. Yeah. . . .' He nodded thoughtfully. 'One wagon could do it easy. I could send the other rigs back south to our headquarters. Two drivers is all we would need to get you two and your gear to Klamath Falls.'

'You say it would be fairly fast run?' said Liam.

'Fast enough.' Maddox nodded. 'You would be surprised how much speed can be cussed out of an ornery Texas steer.'

'The big question is,' said Wayne, 'can the Humboldt be forded anywhere hereabouts?'

'Well now,' grunted Maddox. 'That will take some figurin' out.' He bellowed to Uncle Jack Munson and Philip Mitchell, who were playing checkers in the shade of a harness shack some short distance away. 'Uncle Jack, your rheumatics quit achin' yet?'

'Quit achin' around sun up today,' came the old man's terse reply.

'That is important,' Maddox solemnly explained to the Buford brothers. 'Yeah, that takes care of the weather. There will be no more rain over the next three, maybe four days, which means the river will drop down some. Might even drop low enough for us to take a chance and ford at Apple Grove tomorrow mornin'.'

'You can come to such a conclusion,' Wayne eyed him in surprise, and with some amusement, 'just by enquiring about the old man's rheumatism?'

'Don't sell Uncle Jack short,' drawled Maddox. 'His rheumatism always was reliable.' He yelled to Philip Mitchell, 'Hey, Philip! Saddle a horse and go try a crossin'.'

Without a word of complaint or dissent, Philip abandoned the checkers game, entered the shack and reappeared hefting a saddle and bridle.

'Whichaway?' was all he asked.

'Over by Apple Grove ought to be the best place,' said Maddox. 'And I got five dollars says you don't get back before noon.'

'That money,' drawled Philip, 'is as good as in my pocket.'

'What exactly will Philip do?' Liam, the younger Buford brother, enquired of Maddox.

'There is a place where the river flows broad a ways west of Cosby's Gorge,' Maddox answered directly. 'Apple Grove Crossing, we call it. As good a place as any I can think of, and we would save a heap of time. If Claude Butterworth aims to better not be in any hurry to make Oregon. I figure it is faster and easier to ford at Apple Grove. Anyways, Philip will give it a go.'

'A . . . go ?' Liam blinked. 'But damn it all, Maddox, if the current is running too strong—'

'Philip,' nodded Maddox, 'could get washed clear off his horse's back.'

'Can he swim?' demanded the elder Buford brother.

Glen Maddox grinned wryly.

'No call for you to fret, Mr Buford. Philip taught the fish how to swim,' Maddox said with a wink. 'Or so he claims.'

He took his ease on the top rail with the brothers, enjoying his cigar and lending an attentive ear to their story. Until just a few months ago, they had both worked for the biggest of the Arizona newspapers, the *Phoenix Democratic Chronicle*. Wayne was assistant to the editor, Liam was a typesetter. They had been saving their pay, yearning for the day when they could travel north to Oregon and settle in Klamath Falls, a town largely populated by Bufords,

McCandles, Wymans and Bentons, all members of the Buford clan. They had hoped too, to become the founders of Klamath Falls' first newspaper. But, of course, such a project would call for ample capital, and the brothers weren't exactly overpaid for their services to the Phoenix Democratic Chronicle.

Then came the day when Wayne Buford took his courage in both hands, drew every dollar of his savings out of the Phoenix Community Bank and bought into a high-stake poker game. By sundown, he had tripled his savings. Brother Liam contributed all his own bankroll to that held by Wayne, and Wayne began betting heavily – and still winning. When that long session at last came to an end, the Bufords had their stake, not a king's ransom, not a fortune, but more than enough for the realization of their dream. They could afford to travel to Oregon in style, to rent suitable premises in Klamath Falls, to install their newly purchased equipment and get to work on the project so dear to their hearts.

'The *Klamath Falls Observer*,' Wayne assured Maddox, 'will be a friendly paper and democratic. There will be no muck-raking, no partisan attitude when elections are held, no criticism that isn't richly deserved. The dignity of the individual, and of the entire community, will be upheld at all times.'

'Let the big city tabloids take sides,' muttered Liam. 'A frontier journal should steer the middle course.'

'You gents got some mighty fine notions,' Maddox conceded. 'If I ever sight a copy of the *Klamath Falls*

Observer, I will buy it and read every line – and that is a promise.' And now he thought to ask, 'Can either of you take a turn at drivin' four spans of mules?'

'I am afraid not.' Wayne chuckled. 'A pair of docile mares hitched to a surrey is as much as we can handle.'

'Well, no matter.' Maddox shrugged. 'You are payin' for the freightin', so you oughtn't have to take a turn at drivin'.'

'One of your rigs should be ample,' opined Liam, staring towards the stalled wagons. 'Are they as strong as they look?'

'Stronger,' said Maddox. 'These wagons were built special for totin' freight – a lot of freight, and most of it heavy stuff.'

'The four crates and our personal baggage,' mused Wayne. 'Uh-huh.' He nodded agreement. 'I would say you are right, Liam. One wagon would do.'

'Can't promise you will travel as soft as in a railroad car,' warned Maddox. 'Only one seat in a freight wagon, and that is where the driver sits.'

'We will manage, Maddox,' Wayne Buford assured him.

Of the freight charges he had collected from several local wholesalers on Saturday, Maddox had less than fifty dollars left. He consulted his timepiece, dug his wad from his hip pocket and, at exactly eight minutes before noon, peeled off a five dollar bill and held it in readiness between forefinger and thumb, because Philip was riding towards the corral. The horse's legs and belly were still wet, its rider needed a change of clothing; obviously, he had obeyed Maddox's instructions to the letter, testing the force of the current in the old-fashioned way. Ellis Allum came loafing out of one of the other barns to take charge of the winded bay gelding, after Philip climbed to the top rail and accepted the proffered money.

'Made it easy to the north bank and back,' Philip informed them, as he began rolling a cigarette. 'That lil' old river's droppin' gradual. Current's strong but, if it couldn't faze one saddle horse, you can bet a team and rig could make it.'

'That settles it then?' asked Wayne Buford.

'That settles it.' Maddox nodded. 'By mid mornin' tomorrow, the Humboldt will be runnin' lower still – at Apple Grove, anyway. That means the water won't come up any higher than the wagon bed, so your gear will scarce get wet at all. Yep. We will take you to Oregon, gents – baggage, printin' press and all.'

'Fine,' said Wayne. 'I will advise the manager of the railroad depot, arrange for our equipment to be unloaded and—'

'And tell 'em Maddox will be along to load it around 2.30 or three at the latest today,' added Maddox.

The Buford brothers insisted on sealing their contract with the boss freighter by paying him a portion of the agreed upon fee. They then returned to town, visited Claude Butterworth at the railroad depot and told him of their decision to continue their journey north by mule freight. Butterworth was slightly flabbergasted, but was forced to acknowledge, 'Maddox's a reliable man. If he claims he can ford the Humboldt in a mule-drawn wagon, you can bet he already weighed the odds. He is wild but he is nobody's fool, that much is sure.'

Back at the Commercial Hotel, the Bufords wished the desk clerk to have their bill ready after breakfast on the morrow.

'And it will need to be a mighty early breakfast,' the older brother pointed out, 'because Maddox has decided we will leave right after sunrise.'

His inquisitiveness stimulated, the clerk pressed them for more details, and Wayne and Liam Buford had no reason for keeping their plans secret. As for the clerk, he just happened to be a gossip monger. Just a little after one o'clock that day, there were very few of the stranded travelers ignorant of the Bufords' intentions. The majority opined that the brothers 'must be mighty desperate to get to Oregon – if they would travel all that far with mule skinners'. Of course, the majority were prepared to make the most of the situation and accept the alternative trans-portation arranged by the Galveston and Buffalo Bayou, they were in no great hurry. As for the minor-ity. . . .

At about 2.30 in the afternoon, Mena Donahoe was accompanied from the local cemetery by the wife and spinster sister of the clergyman who had con-cluded the funeral service for her murdered father. These good women urged her to join them at the parson's home, insisting that she should not be left to herself at such a trying time, but Mena firmly declined the invitation.

'Thank you both, very much,' she acknowledged. 'I realize you are trying to be kind, and I sincerely appreciate it, but you don't have to worry on my account. If I don't seem completely grief stricken, it is because poor Dad and I had been separated for a long time. I guess,' she shrugged dejectedly, 'I guess I had gotten accustomed to missing him.'

After the well-meaning ladies had walked her back to the hotel and gone on their way, Mena stood on the front porch of the Commercial Hotel, staring across towards the stalled express. There was considerable activity at the train depot. A large wagon to which a mule team was harnessed had been stalled level with the baggage car of the train. Under the supervision of the Buford brothers, several crates were being transferred to the wagon, and this hefty chore was being performed not by the railroad employees but by two of the roughest looking men Mena had ever laid eyes upon. While waiting on tables in the White Pines hash house, she had encountered more than her share of hard cases, but none to compare with these. Glen Maddox and Texas John Quayle were hefting, tugging, shoving the crates as easily as if they contained nothing but feathers.

Myrtle Cross approached from the uptown area, climbed to the porch and stood beside her. For just a few moments, the grandmother-to-be abandoned her customary aggressive demeanor and spoke gently.

'I was there, child. Didn't know your father. We weren't introduced. But I went along anyway, fearing you might be all alone.'

'The wife and sister of the preacher . . .' began Mena.

'Yes.' Myrtle nodded. 'I didn't intrude, because I saw you were in good hands. Well. . . .' She patted Mena's arm. 'I will not burden you with a long speech of sympathy, child. Let me just say that, if there is anything I can do to help, you have only to ask, dear.'

'Thank you,' said Mena.

At that moment, Bettie Erickson emerged from the lobby to join them. She took her cue from the older woman and expressed her sympathy in brevity.

'I would have attended the services,' she assured Mena, 'if it weren't for the children. They have to be watched almost every minute. . . .'

She sighed wearily, brushed the hair from her eyes and sank into a porch chair.

Glancing down at her, Myrtle Cross declared, 'I certainly admire your Christian charity, Miss Erickson, and your stamina. You would need a lot of both – taking on such a chore. Eight frisky, rambunctious youngsters. . . .'

'They are fine children,' said Bettie. 'But like all children, they can be . . . very tiresome.'

'Nobody knows that better that I,' Myrtle warmly asserted. 'I have raised nine of my own, and now I am determined to make sure my eldest gets proper treatment. Her first is due any day now.' She drew her shawl tighter about her plump shoulders, grimaced in exasperation. 'So much delay and so much calamity all at once. A railroad bridge damaged by a bolt of lightning – of all things.'

'Some are calling it an act of God,' suggested Bettie.

'That may be true enough,' Myrtle agreed.

'The children are so terribly disappointed,' murmured Bettie. 'For all but two of them, it was their first train journey. And, of course, they are so eager to get to Laurel Valley – their first real home.' She stared wistfully northward. 'I feel almost as sorry for the good folk who have adopted them. The legalities took so much time. We were on our way at last, and expecting to reach Laurel Valley three days from now. It is a great shame. Mr Butterworth said the journey to the valley by wagon will take almost ten days or two weeks, because of our having to detour by way of Fortson's Ford.'

The women were silent a moment, as they watched the toiling freighters at work.

Myrtle quietly remarked, 'There are times when I am forced to admit that men are resourceful – more resourceful than women. This is one of those times. Look over there.'

'Mr Buford and his brother,' Bettie said.

'They were not content to sit and fret about the problem,' said Myrtle. 'They did something positive, went out and made their own arrangements – independent of the railroad. The younger Mr Buford told me about it at lunch. They are hiring one of the

Maddox wagons to take them to Klamath Falls, Oregon, faster than the rest of us.'

'You said one of the Maddox wagons?' said Mena.

'If it is the same Maddox freight company that travels all over Nevada and California,' said Myrtle, 'there are three wagons in all. Old Galen Maddox and his three wagons, his mules and his mule skinners used to be quite an institution. I understand his son is carrying on the tradition. They will haul freight anywhere – under almost any conditions—' She broke off, frowning at Mena Donahoe. 'You lovely young woman, why do you stare at me?'

'Would it be such a wild idea?' breathed Mena. 'I wonder.'

She held a brief conference with Myrtle Cross and Bettie Erickson and, after their initial surprise, both women expressed agreement with her suggestion. The grandmother-to-be warmly asserted, 'There isn't much I wouldn't do, for the sakes of being with Mary Rose at this time. And that includes bullying the almighty Glen Maddox.'

'I realize those wagons were not built to carry passengers,' said Mena, 'but surely it would be a simple matter to fit some makeshift seats, rig canvas canopies, just like on the Conestogas.'

'It can be done and it will be done,' declared Myrtle Cross. 'Come, ladies. We will strike while the iron is hot.'

Maddox and Texas John had lashed the crates into position and were discussing the question of improvised seating with the Bufords, when the women abruptly arrived. Wayne Buford courteously performed introductions. The freighters doffed their hats. Maddox said, 'Proud to meet you, ladies—'

And that was as much as he was permitted to say, for almost five minutes. When it came to stating a case, making a request or putting a proposition, Myrtle Cross was as tough, wily and tenacious as any horse trader. Once or twice, Maddox tried to interject. It just did not work. Myrtle would not be silent until she had said her piece – all of it.

'Three wagons – ample space,' she concluded. 'I happen to know you finished a haul right here in Battle Mountain, Mr Maddox, and that means your other rigs are empty and idle. The Galveston and Buffalo Bayou is bound to refund a fair proportion of our fare. You will be paid a reasonable fee for your services, and all we ask is that you have seating accommodation fitted to your wagons as quickly as possible. We will supply provisions and cook for your drivers as well as the children.'

'It is in a very good cause, Mr Maddox,' Bettie earnestly assured him. 'These unfortunate orphans – on their way to their first real home. . . .'

Maddox and Texas John stood beside the wagon, stunned, jolted and a mite incredulous, not to mention thoroughly intimidated by the aggressive Myrtle Cross. The Buford brothers traded frowns and wisely refrained from comment. Hat in hand, and resisting the impulse to punctuate his speech with profanity, Glen Maddox endeavored to convince the ladies.

'What you are askin' just can't be done. Our rigs were never meant for totin' women and children. The mules would likely get mighty nervous and so would my drivers.'

'Stop dickering, Mr Maddox,' chided Myrtle. 'We know you are willing to carry passengers to Klamath Falls.'

'Only two of 'em.' Maddox nodded to the Buford brothers. 'And both men. No females.'

'Miss Donahoe is bound for Stag Ridge,' said Myrtle. 'You have to cross Stag Ridge anyway, don't you?'

'Well, sure.' He nodded. 'The Klamath Falls trail cuts through Deerhorn Pass.'

'Deerhorn Pass!' Mena nodded eagerly. 'That is where my fiancé will be. Oh, please, Mr Maddox! I would be no trouble at all. I have very little baggage. And – and I would be willing to make myself useful. I can cook and sew. . . .'

'What about the children?' Myrtle asked. 'They want to travel to Laurel Valley, which happens to be only a little way north of Stag Ridge, and directly on the route to Klamath Falls.'

'But—' began Glen Maddox.

'Do you or do you not have to travel through Laurel Valley?' challenged Myrtle.

'Well, sure,' shrugged Maddox, 'but—'

'And,' Myrtle finished triumphantly, 'my daughter and her husband live in the settlement of Evansburg. You would have to go by way of Evansburg anyway, because it is located right close to Evans Creek.'

'You see . . . the trouble is—' Maddox desperately tried again.

'You would water your animals at Evans Creek, wouldn't you?' demanded Myrtle.

'Yeah, we would, sure,' said Maddox. 'But . . .'

'Then why waste time in pointless argument?' she chided the freighter. 'If one wagon can ford the river at Apple Grove tomorrow morning, it would be just as easy for all three. You need only rig a few planks for seating, and load our baggage in back. We could be across the border and into Oregon by Tuesday night.'

Bettie took over. While Texas John stood mute, gulping on the lump in his throat, the fragile spinster told Maddox of the eight orphans adopted by the good folk of Laurel Valley. Maddox grimaced uneasily, fidgeted in acute discomfort.

And then, when Bettie had finished speaking, Mena put a hand on Maddox's brawny arm, stared up into his battered countenance and tore away the last shreds of his resistance.

'There will surely come a day,' she vowed, 'when you will be planning your own marriage. Could you bear to be separated from the woman you love? Well, that is how it is for Antone and me. He is all I have left, now that my father is gone. . . .'

She talked on for a few more moments. When Maddox next managed to get a word in edgeways, it was only to say, 'If you ladies will have someone from the hotel staff stash your gear on the depot platform, we will be along and get it loaded before sundown.'

96

'There!' Myrtle Cross smiled complacently at Mena and Bettie. 'I told you Mr Maddox would listen to reason.'

'Just one thing,' said Maddox, as the women made to leave. 'Be sure to bring plenty of cotton.'

'I'm sorry, cotton?' Mena eyed him uncomprehendingly.

'For your ears,' he explained, 'and for the kids, too. Mules won't hustle 'less we cuss at them, and it wouldn't be fittin' for ladies and young'uns to hear such language.'

After the women had returned to the hotel, Wayne Buford stared hard at Maddox and opined, 'You have taken on quite a responsibility and maybe Liam and I are partly to blame. When we mentioned hiring one of your rigs while talking to Mrs Cross. . . .'

'I swear we never believed she would get the same notion,' muttered Liam.

'Ain't no fault of yours, gents,' drawled Texas John. 'Maddox could have said no – only he never learned how, you see?'

'We will tote this load back,' Maddox decided. 'Best pass the word to the boys pronto, get some planks rigged for the women and children to sit on.'

He bade the Bufords a temporary farewell and climbed up beside the Texan. They cussed the mules, the mules leaned against their harness and the wagon rumbled away along Main Street, headed for the northern outskirts. Maddox let his sidekick take the reins, while he rolled and lit a cigarette and did some deep thinking about the territory between

Battle Mountain, Nevada and Klamath Falls, Oregon.

The route presented no difficulties that he could think of offhand; he had led his outfit that far north many a time. But this time would be different – and then some.

'I must be out of my gosh darn mind,' he complained, 'lettin' myself get roped into such a deal.'

'Boy,' grunted Texas John, 'you will get no arguments from me.'

Maddox lapsed into a moody silence. He had a thoughtful side; his life wasn't entirely made up of hauling freight, roistering, brawling, pursuing nothing but his own pleasure, in many ways he was as much a pioneer as any settler, prospector, cattleman, nester or backwoods preacher, because he had followed in the steps of his father, helping to open up the unchartered vastness of the West.

Also, he wasn't quite as carefree a hell-raiser as he appeared to be. His hired help were like members of his own family. There were no blood-ties, but the younger men were like brothers to him, and Old Jack Munson had been 'Uncle Jack' for as far back as he could remember.

And now his responsibilities were to increase more than somewhat. The Maddox outfit was about to tote passengers as well as freight, after all these years. Three women, two men, eight children. Holy smoke!

One of those women – Mena Donahoe – now returned to her room at the Commercial Hotel and, with a thrill of alarm, discovered that her bag had been searched during her absence.

CHAPTER 7

FOLLOW THE MONEY

Mena Donahoe locked the doors before re-checking her possessions to confirm her distrust. She could clearly recall that her carpet bag had been placed directly in the corner nearest the door. It was still there, but its position had changed ever so slightly, but noticeably. She went to the bag, opened it and checked the contents. Nothing had been taken, but she was still sure, very sure, that the bag had been combed through. The few clothes she had unpacked had been shifted in the drawer of the dresser; additionally, the lasting odor of cigar smoke indicated the room had been entered and the prowler had remained longer than mere minutes. She even detected a few grayish smears of cigar ash on the rug.

Standing by the window, she stared uptown in the

general direction of the sheriff's office and struggled with her surreptitious thoughts. How would the local law enforcement react, if the daughter of ex-convict Hugh Donahoe lodged such a complaint? 'I am certain somebody broke into my room. No, nothing was stolen, but they were looking for something as my bag was rummaged through.'

The sheriff would investigate, and an investigation would unquestionably mean a postponement; she might be prohibited from leaving town tomorrow morning. Better to say nothing of the occurrence. But who had picked the lock to her room and searched it and her bag – and more importantly – what were they looking for? Did she dress in such a manner that would give would-be robbers the impression she had money? Hardly. Why then? The question would remain unanswered unless the unknown trespassers paid her a second visit. She resolved to accept the offer extended by the maternal Myrtle Cross.

'If you think you will feel lonely tonight, just say the word and I will keep you company. It would not be the first time I have slept on a sofa to comfort a fretting child.'

Upstairs in the room shared by Clay Parker and Peter Vogel, another council of war was being held. Frank Humes was reporting, 'I checked every last damn inch of that room. The bag, the dresser – everything, I tell you. If Donahoe's daughter got that loot off him, she sure didn't hide it in her room.'

'She must have it!' glowered Parker. He was rested

on the window sill, chewing on an unlit cigar. 'There is no other explanation. He couldn't have hidden it in his own baggage, so he planted it in his daughter's. Don't forget they were big bills, so it didn't add up to a hefty bundle. It could all be packed under the base of a carpet bag or inside the lining of a valise.'

'She don't have no valise, and I checked that carpet bag careful,' acknowledged Humes.

'How about the gowns in her closet?' prompted James Kruse.

'Yep, searched them too,' said a growingly frustrated Humes.

Kruse snapped his fingers and shook his head.

'Wait a darn minute! The trunk!'

'There was a trunk?' Parker showed quick interest now.

'Her trunk,' said Kruse. 'We saw it loaded into the baggage car at White Pines. Should have thought of it before, Clay. That is the only place Donahoe could have stashed the stuff.'

'Sure, I recall it now,' muttered Carl Gobson. 'It was a sizeable trunk – about so big.' He had his arms extended out from side to side.

'Green, it was,' said Kruse. 'With her name on one side.'

He eyed Parker keenly. 'Well, Clay? What do you think?'

'It has to be the trunk,' said Parker. 'Hell, we have tried everywhere else.'

'The question is,' agonized Peter Vogel, 'is how do

101

we get to that trunk? We would have to bust the lock, and. . . .'

'The answer is we don't get to the trunk,' moped Parker. 'At least not here in town. That baggage car has been sealed and guarded since the Buford brothers had their freight unloaded. Sometime between now and tomorrow, they will have to unload it all – including the Donahoe girl's trunk – and pack it onto wagons bound for Fortson's Ford.'

'So?' tested Levi Ward, who up until that moment had just listened but said nothing.

'So,' exhaled Parker, 'wherever that trunk goes, we go too.'

For some substantial time, thereafter, the survivors of the Tulley gang continued their discussion of the large green trunk bearing the name 'Donahoe'. There was no argument. All six were convinced of the correctness of Kruse's intuition; the missing $75,000 just had to be hidden in that trunk.

'Donahoe had time enough, I reckon,' Kruse was saying. 'Time enough to get to his daughter's trunk, peel off some of the lining or maybe lay a false bottom in it. That is not too hard a thing to do. He could have stashed the money in the trunk sometime between givin' us the slip in White Pines and checkin' out the railroad hotel to board the train.'

'One thing I am curious about,' muttered Gobson. 'Does the girl know about the money? Did her old man let her in on his secret or was he playin' his cards close to the vest?'

'We can't be sure about that,' shrugged Parker, 'either way.'

'She is old enough to read a newspaper,' snarled Ward. 'She knows why her pappy served five years at the Fort.'

'Well,' Parker said, 'there will be two of us traveling along with the buckboards and wagons – whatever rigs the railroad hires to ship the passengers to the ford. The rest of us will tag along to keep an eye on them and, when I give the word, we will move in.'

'Easy pickin's,' smirked Gobson. 'There will be no guards. Just the hired drivers.'

'Grabbing that trunk beyond the county limits,' drawled Parker, 'will certainly be a damn sight safer than trying to grab it here in town.' Gobson made to offer another rejoinder, but Parker raised his hand for silence.

He was staring intently towards the railroad depot. Two hefty wagons – both mule-drawn – had been driven level with the baggage car. More boxes were being transferred from the baggage car to the freight wagons, with all of Maddox's roughneck crew applying themselves to the task.

Parker's voice shook a little. 'I don't like this,' he muttered. 'You said a green trunk. . . ?'

'Yeah, that's right, green,' said Gobson, nodding. 'About yay big. . . .'

'They are unloading it now,' growled Parker. 'Stashing it in a damn-blasted freight wagon.'

'How many wagons?' called Ward.

'Only two,' replied Parker.

'Well, damn it all,' grimaced Kruse, 'they would need more than two wagons to tote all the baggage off that train.'

'The way it looks to me,' countered Parker, 'they aren't unloading all the baggage. Only some of it – including that Donahoe girl's.' He turned and nodded to Kruse. 'Go on down there, James. As a passenger, you have a right to be curious. Ask a question or two. I want to know exactly what is happening.'

Half an hour later, when James Kruse re-entered the room, his face appeared forbidding. It had not been at all difficult for him to learn of the alternative transportation secured by the three women and eight children; the desk clerk had already made up their bills and was as loquacious as ever.

'Gettin' that trunk,' he scowled, 'ain't gonna be so damn easy, after all, is it?'

'Why not?' Parker impatiently demanded.

Kruse answered his question with another.

'You ever hear of the Maddox outfit?'

'Everybody knows the Maddox outfit,' said Parker, frowning. 'You might as well ask if I have heard of Wells Fargo or Western Union or. . .' His voice trailed off. A flush stole over his usually ashen expression and he clenched his fists and teeth. 'Hold on now, James! Are you telling me. . .?'

'It is for sure.' Kruse nodded. 'The trunk will be headed north – not east – tomorrow mornin'. Maddox's been hired to tote the Donahoe girl, two other females and a bunch of kids up into Oregon and all their baggage.'

'The whole Maddox outfit!' Clay Parker's eyes shone.

'Maddox's old man is dead and gone now,' said Kruse, 'but I have heard it said his son is three times as tough, and he is bossin' a right wild bunch. What are we gonna do, Clay? If we have to fight seven real salty guns.'

'Nine, maybe,' suggested Ward, 'iffen those Buford brothers lend a hand, I reckon.'

'I want my share of that money,' growled Gobson, 'but I don't like the odds. Nine against the six of us. The hell with that – we could be wiped out.'

Parker turned away from the window, helped himself to a chair. A nerve twitched at his temple. His face was contorted, his voice reduced to a husky, impassioned whisper.

'There has to be an easier way. No risk to ourselves – and the certainty of being able to open that trunk and search it at our leisure. As for Maddox and his friends, they would never see us and they would never know what hit them.'

'You mean we would play it sneaky – hit 'em at night, perhaps?' suggested Ward.

'I mean we wouldn't need to get within range of them,' said Parker. 'For a few kegs of cheap whiskey, I could persuade somebody else to take care of those sharp-shooting freighters.'

'Cheap whiskey?' Levi Ward frowned in disgust at the very notion. 'Aw, hell, Clay. You wouldn't. . . .'

'What is the matter, Levi?' scoffed Parker. 'You aren't turnin' soft on me, are you?'

'The Northern Paiute Indians signed a treaty several years ago,' Ward reminded him. 'You got any notion what a few kegs of firewater would do to those savages? They would go kill crazy. If all the Northern Paiute tribes go on the warpath again. . . .'

They were all aware of the fragile treaty with the Paiute. The treaty had been broken on several occasions, the last being when a white man – Dexter Demming – had been murdered when his home was raided. His brother, Jack, had once killed a Paiute Indian and this was retribution. The governor had directed the army to meet with the Paiute leader to honor the treaty and turn over the killers. But both sides and all in the area expected a larger war was looming.

'I'm not thinking of every stinking Indian on the Owens Pines reservation,' grinned Parker, 'I'm only thinking of Tocho and his pals. About seventy or eighty of 'em. Maybe a hundred, not more than that. They could do it, Levi. And I know where to find Tocho. Where to find him, how to talk to him, how to nudge him into a raid on those freighters. Tocho can't handle his whiskey. A couple mouthfuls and he thirsts for more and more. If I promise him a whole dozen kegs or so . . . watch out. . . .'

'Yeah, that would do it.' Ward sighed. 'That would be enough reason for that wild savage Tocho to paint his ugly face for killin'.'

'I would warn him against using fire arrows,'

106

drawled Parker. 'There will be no burning so the loot will be safe.'

'No burning,' grunted Ward. 'Just killin' women and children as well as Maddox and his whole outfit.'

'This is no time to get squeamish,' mumbled Vogel, with the perspiration streaming down his face. 'Damn it all, Levi, have you ever sat down and tallied your share – a sixth of $75,000? That's. . . .' He licked his lips and averted his eyes. 'That is better that 12,000. A lot of money, Levi.'

'A man could live high and easy for quite a long spell,' mused Humes, 'with that amount of money behind him.'

'And we have waited a long time for that money,' muttered Gobson.

'Tomorrow,' announced Parker, 'we will give Maddox ample time to get clear of the county. Then we will hire a couple of packhorses, invest some of our own coin in whiskey and go pay Tocho a little social visit. I happen to know where his bunch are and the army's been hunting them ever since. Well, the army could not find them but I sure can.'

CHAPTER 8

A STUDY IN CONTRASTS

A great many Battle Mountain citizens turned out to view the exodus of the northbound Maddox outfit around ten o'clock in the following morning – a remarkable sight, a study in contrasts. The personal belongings of the three women and eight children were packed into the rear sections of the second and third wagons. Behind the drivers' seats had been rigged two extra seats to accommodate the travelers. The canopies of patched canvas had been raised. Stalled there, with the ugly mules harnessed and waiting, those vehicles appeared none too appealing to all save the small children, who were chuckling with excitement, as the burly freighters lifted them aboard. The first wagon, with Uncle Jack and Texas John on the seat, the Buford brothers perched behind them and their baggage and equipment stowed in back, was stalled outside the next building uptown.

Maddox had saddled one of the horses, the bay gelding. It stood hitched to the hotel rack, while he supervised the loading of the baggage and assigned the passengers to their wagons. Miss Erickson and her small charges were to occupy the second rig. With Myrtle Cross for company, Mena Donahoe would travel in the third.

There was clamor, activity, eagerness, but no confusion; the routine of departure proceeded without undue delay. Locals lined the boardwalks to wave farewell, to wish the northbound travelers good fortune. As for the study in contrasts, there was irony in the spectacle of the mule-drawn wagons – those enormous and clumsy-looking vehicles – lumbering up the main street of Battle Mountain, while the bright and shining locomotive with its three smartly painted carriages (the pride of the Galveston and Buffalo Bayou railroad) remained motionless at the railroad depot, unable to continue the journey north.

Beyond Battle Mountain, the freighters found that the regular trail had become fairly firm; the heat of the sun was intense, so that the muddy conditions caused by Saturday's storm no longer existed. It was safe for the drivers to urge their mule teams to the utmost speed, and they did that – to the discomfort of the ladies, but to the great delight of the children.

With Battle Mountain a full three miles to their

rear, they eased the pace, settling to the steady trot that would guarantee their reaching the border in record time. Maddox, tall and formidable in the saddle of the bay, the sun gleaming off the well-worn butt of the .45 slung to his right hip, was already becoming comfortable to the chore of shipping humans as well as freight. He rode level with the second rig a while; trading polite talk with the elderly but courageous spinster who had undertaken the task of delivering eight active youngsters to the community of their foster parents. The children barraged him with question after question, all of which he answered to the best of his ability with good humor.

He slowed the bay gelding a little, waited for the third wagon to catch up, then began riding level with it. Philip Mitchell and Jacob Maher were on the front seat, Philip driving.

'Chances are,' Jacob called to his boss-freighter, 'the river will be low enough for an easy crossin' if it stays this hot.'

'I swear I can feel the land dryin' out,' drawled Philip.

'Better than drivin' through mud, huh, Philip?' said Maddox.

'That is for damn sure,' agreed Philip.

Maddox doffed his Stetson to Mena and Myrtle, both of whom had unfurled their parasols.

'You ladies comfortable?' he asked them.

'We are managing,' Mena assured him.

'No use complaining,' warned Myrtle, 'about a few

bumps and bruises.'

He rode at ease, one leg hooked about his saddle horn, as he rolled and lit a cigarette.

'You said your man will be waitin' for us at Deerhorn Pass?' Maddox asked Mena.

'I paid the desk clerk back at the hotel, to wire Antone today,' she said. 'Antone will calculate the time it will take us to reach the pass and, when we do, he will be waiting for us.' She thought to add, 'If you need any help in the Stag Ridge country – repairs to the wagon, feed for the mules, anything like that – I am sure Antone would be glad to help. He has a lot of influence in that territory.'

'You sound plumb proud of him, Miss Mena.' Maddox nodded approvingly. 'Well, that is the way it ought to be. And I will bet he is just as proud of you.'

'Her man,' offered Myrtle, 'is in the lumber business.'

'Sounds fine,' said Maddox. 'In Oregon, lumber is the most important business of all, so I hear.'

The traveling was easier than he had anticipated. Philip and Jacob joined in the conversation, and the women did not seem to mind. Myrtle Cross, despite her unfriendly exterior, soon proved herself to be more an asset than a liability. By noon, she had transferred to the second wagon to help Bettie tend a travel-sick kid and had bullied Jacob Maher into producing his spare shirt, which was badly in need of patching. Having patched Jacob's shirt, she whispered a suggestion to Mena. They filled a bowl with water, borrowed jack-knives from Philip and Jacob,

111

and began peeling a large quantity of potatoes. For the mule skinners, the midday meal was somewhat more substantial than usual. Uncle Jack's cook fire was invaded by the three women, plus extra pots and more rations. The old man was as cantankerous as ever, but not with the women and children. He sternly ordered his colleagues to keep their distance.

'While me and the ladies – I mean the ladies and me – rustle up the best durn chow you ever tasted.'

It was a fine-looking spread, and the freighters were beyond feeling obstinate or ill at ease in the presence of these women. The children, with all the poignant readiness of the very young, were already referring to these rough men as Uncle Philly, Uncle Ellis, and Uncle Jake. Like children the world over, they would accept and identify any grown up as a protector on whom they could always rely. All it took, to establish and cement this relationship, was for Texas John to show one tiny girl how to dance a waltz, Texas style, while Ellis Allum blew a discordant tune from a harmonica; or for Claus Becker to spin tall tales for a small audience of three, all about his adventures as a prospector, 'Digging for purple glass in the Big Boulder Mountains, back in the magical Fairyland, when I was only seven years old – it is the truth!'; or for Glen Maddox to permit a glowing eyed boy to ride the bay gelding 'for an entire twenty-five whole yards all by his own self'.

A much-relieved Mena Donahoe took her place in the third wagon for the resumption of the journey. Eager to be reunited with the man she loved, she had nevertheless felt some disquiet about this alternative transportation, the prospect of travelling so many miles over lonely territory in the company of seven very rough men. In the past five years, she had come to know and to understand the opposite sex, their weaknesses, their capacity for cruelty, the predatory instinct that compelled so many frontiersmen to take advantage of a pretty waitress in a cheap hash house. Maintaining her respectability had been somewhat of a struggle – she had one epic memory of being forced to protect herself with a frying pan. The pan had been bent beyond repair, her would-be lover was sprawled senseless on the floor of the hash house kitchen with an egg-sized bump on his head, and Mena's virginity was intact. The proprietor had threatened to fire her, because such violence was apt to antagonize the paying customers.

At first, Maddox's ready grin and slightly posses-sive demeanor had caused her some alarm. Now, she recognized his attitude for what it was, the easy and uninhibited attitude of a man without flirtation, friendliness that was warm, but platonic, never pas-sionate, never demanding. To travel under the protection of Maddox and his colleagues was like traveling with six older brothers and one aged uncle.

The fording of the Humboldt River at Apple Grove was accomplished without mishap. By the time they reached that broad waterway, some thirty minutes after breaking noon camp, the level of the river had dropped to almost normal. Maddox forded astride the bay, all the time testing for the best course

113

for the wagons. He then returned to the south bank, following exactly the same course and with his drivers watching intently, memorizing the turns he had made.

'OK underneath, huh?' jabbed Uncle Jack.

'The bay made it twice and no strain,' Maddox pointed out, 'which means those mules ought to do it easy as well. All right, amigos, let's go.'

'Me first!' Uncle Jack yelled over his shoulder. 'Hit the river, Mad-dox, and away we go. . . .'

The children squealed with excitement as the first rig was hauled into the water by the struggling, snorting mules. Uncle Jack cracked his whip. Texas John unleashed an ear-splitting whoop, while the brothers Buford clung to their seat and traded philosophical grins. In a little under ten minutes or so, the mules, two mule skinners, the future owners of the *Klamath Falls Observer* and the all-important printing press had made it safely to the north bank.

'Go, Ellis!' called Maddox.

'Mad-doooox!' wailed Ellis Allum.

He cracked his whip and the second rig, with the children clustered together and laughing, and Bettie Erickson hugging the youngest to her bosom and fervently praying, lurched forward to begin fording. Mena and Myrtle rose in the third rig to watch, as Maddox again put his bay gelding into the river. All the way to the north bank, the boss freighter stayed level with the wagon containing the children, yelling encouragement to Ellis and Claus, joking with the children to distract their attention from the roaring of the water, the squawking of the mules and the imaginative cussing of the driver, and flashing many a reassuring grin at the tensed-up Bettie. But not until that heavy-laden wagon was rolling to a halt on level ground did the elderly spinster relax. She sighed so loud that the sound clearly reached Maddox, who assured her.

'It wasn't half as dangerous as it felt. You just take it easy now, ma'am. Relax. You may now breathe,' he said with a smile.

'I thought for sure we would overturn and be drowned,' she confided. 'The way the water seemed to buffet us. . . .'

'This old river always hits hard,' said Maddox, 'but our wagons are plumb hefty, in case you haven't noticed.'

He rose in his stirrups, cupped his hands about his mouth and yelled to Philip and Jacob. His voice carried clear across the rushing waters, all the way to the south bank, and he didn't call an order. To Bettie Erickson – as she clapped her hands to her ears – it seemed the mule skinners used the name 'Maddox' for any and all purposes. It could mean that food was ready for the eating. It could mean 'let's go' or 'beware' or 'yes, boss', or almost anything at all. Probably its constant usage was all part of some mysterious patois known only to the mule skinners.

'Mad-dox!' yelled Maddox.

And Jacob slapped his team with the reins, while Philip cracked the whip and whooped, and the last team plodded into the Humboldt. Over his shoulder,

Philip politely advised Mena and Myrtle to 'Grab onta somethin' and hold on tight, ladies, and don't you worry about nothin'.'

'You aren't afraid, child?' Myrtle solicitously enquired, as she cast a glance at the fast-moving waters.

'We saw the other wagons get across just fine,' shrugged Mena, 'so I guess we have nothing to worry about.'

The rig lurched slightly. One mule floundered and, for a brief moment, its head was submerged.

'That looks like Marty,' remarked Philip Mitchell. 'And I recall he is a mite shy of water.'

'It ain't Marty,' grunted Jacob. 'It is Mr Longears and he don't relish a bath no more than Marty does.'

'That damn fool critter better rise up fast,' preached Philip, 'else he is apt to drown.'

'He's up,' announced Jacob, as the momentarily submerged mule's head broke the surface.

'That's good,' drawled Philip. 'I was always partial to Mr Longears. He is stupid but likeable.'

'Reminds me of someone,' joked Jacob, eying his driving partner. The remark went without reply.

The third rig made it to the far bank, and the journey north continued a while. From atop a rise to the southwest, Clay Parker followed the progress of the freighters through high-powered field glasses.

CHAPTER 9

FORDING THE RIVER, THE ENEMY ATTACKS

Returning the binoculars to his saddle bag, Parker traded stares with his five cohorts, and declared, 'If they can cross the river, so can we.'

'Yeah,' said Humes. 'I saw Maddox ford it two or three times.'

Parker called a command to Vogel and Gobson, both of whom were leading laden packhorses.

'Watch those pack animals carefully while we are fording. We can't afford to lose either of 'em.'

'That is a fact,' chuckled Kruse. 'You would surely ruffle Tocho's headdress without whiskey to bargain with.'

They descended from the southwest rise and

moved onto the south bank of the Humboldt River. The fording was slow and cautious; not until mid-stream did the horses show signs of alarm. Urged on by the vehement oaths of their riders, they struggled through the mire and the pounding waters, onto the less violent and shallower sections and, finally, up onto the north bank. Parker dismounted for a careful inspection of the supplies slung to the pack animals. Every keg was still lashed securely into position. He checked every knot before remounting.

'All right,' he grunted. 'From here, we head northwest of the regular trail. There is not much danger those freighters could spot us. And, by tomorrow's sundown, we should be moving through Palisade Canyon.'

'That is where we will find Tocho and his band?' asked Carl Gobson, as the boss outlaw remounted. 'For sure?'

They traveled away from the river in a north westerly direction. Clay Parker took the lead, with James Kruse riding abreast.

'I have always wondered,' Kruse told him, 'how in tarnation you ever got to learn the Paiute lingo.'

'It wasn't easy,' drawled Parker, 'but I stayed with it until I could make myself understand, and savvy most of what they were saying. I had my reasons, James. When a man has strong enough reasons, he can apply himself to damn near any chore, including how to parley with an Indian.'

Kruse said nearly a half an hour later, 'You better be sure this Indian understands what he has to do.

No fire-arrows this time, Clay.'

'No.' Parker's mouth set in a hard line. 'I would hate to see Miss Donahoe's trunk damaged by fire.'

'But Maddox and his sidekicks . . .' began Kruse.

'I would say their chances of survival are about a hundred to one,' said Parker. 'They will be killed. Tocho will take the women and keep them for a while at least. As for the kids, who knows for sure? It will depend on Tocho's mood.'

'Twenty whites could get wiped out,' mused Kruse.

'The alternative,' countered Parker, 'is for us to forget about that $75,000, forget what we have been waiting for these past five years. Does that thought appeal to you, James?'

'Hell, no,' scowled Kruse. 'I crave what is rightfully mine . . . at least what I helped to steal.'

'So,' shrugged Parker, 'don't be like Levi. Don't get squeamish at the idea of a minor massacre.'

Night camp presented no embarrassing problems to the northbound freighters and their passengers. Almost an hour before sundown, Maddox chose the campsite, a well sheltered glen close by the north bank of a clear creek. That water was as clear and as clean as they had ever known, ideal for cooking and for bathing.

The women didn't say as much, but Maddox sensed their desire to take this opportunity of bathing.

'Keeping them clean,' Bettie Erickson complained, 'is an almost impossible chore.'

119

'Who ever heard of a permanently clean young'un?' chuckled Myrtle Cross. 'All right now, Bettie. Get a hustle on, and Mena and I will give you a hand. We will have these little terrors bathed and dried quicker than you can wink.'

Maddox intruded, clearing his throat self-consciously, hefting a sawn-off shotgun. Solemnly, he passed the weapon to the frowning Myrtle.

'Beggin' your pardon, ladies,' he said, 'but I'm guessin' you all hanker for a bath. Well, I guarantee my crew will behave like gentlemen and stay well clear of this part of the creek but you will likely feel a sight easier if you got a little protection close handy.'

Just as solemnly, Myrtle accepted the shotgun.

'Mr Maddox,' she declared, 'you aren't half as wild and thoughtless as you pretend to be.'

'My father used to say,' Maddox recalled, 'a brain is for thinkin' with.'

'He must have been a fine man,' offered Bettie, who felt she should contribute a word of appreciation.

'He was an ornery, hard-drinkin', rock-fisted old hellion that got drunk Saturday nights and ate his meal off the knife,' Maddox told her. He shrugged, heaved a sentimental sigh. 'Yeah, he sure appealed to folks. Everybody admired him.'

For the first time since the untimely demise of her father, Mena burst into laughter; she couldn't restrain herself. Even the aggressive Myrtle was unable to suppress a chuckle. Bettie – she of the prim and sheltered background – didn't quite know what to say or what to think.

'Maddox,' Mena said, 'you are as wonderful as your father must have been, and you make me grateful that I am marrying a good-humored man. You remind me so much of my Antone.'

'Aw, come on, now,' protested Maddox. 'A pretty little lady like you couldn't cotton to an hombre as homely as me.'

'I didn't mean your appearance.' Mena smiled. 'I was referring to your character, and the way you express yourself. Antone's of Irish extraction – tall like you – and whimsical.'

'And he has got good taste,' Maddox gallantly asserted.

By five o'clock the following afternoon, immediately after entering Palisade Canyon, Clay Parker led his group away from the canyon's eastern gateway and into the concealment of a clump of trees.

'Unless that Indian Tocho has decided to migrate,' he announced, 'we are less than a half hour's ride from his camp.'

'All right then,' said Carl Gobson. 'Why don't we go on then?'

'Take whiskey to those bucks tonight,' Parker grinned mirthlessly, 'and they will be good for nothing tomorrow. It takes a Northern Paiute – or any Indian – quite a while to sleep off a drink. Better we should visit him in the morning, give him a few kegs to wet his appetite with a promise of more, after the Maddox outfit has been wiped out. Get off-saddled, boys, and forget about lighting a fire.'

It was characteristic of Clay Parker that he should sleep at ease that night, his conscience untroubled. He was single-minded in his determination to retrieve the loot lost five years ago, after the Sheep Springs affair, and his attitude was shared by his cronies. Levi Ward was ill at ease, badly unsettled at the thought of seventy or more whiskey-crazed 'red devils' – as he called them – being hurled at the unsuspecting freighters like so many wild animals; even so, he craved his share of the stolen cash, as did the apprehensive Peter Vogel.

In the morning, Parker ordered that both pack-horses should be left concealed in the timber. Three kegs only would be presented to Tocho and his band at the start. If all went well, they would reveal to the Northern Paiute the location of the two packhorses and the cache of whiskey.

When they began their ride along the floor of the thickly-wooden Palisade Canyon, Parker was hefting one keg in the crook of his left arm. Kruse and Humes toted the others. They traveled almost a mile before Parker's probing eyes fastened on the lookout away to their left, a buckskinned brave in the act of descending from the summit of a rock mound. The brave froze, startled at being addressed in his own tongue. Having already been warned by Parker, his men wisely refrained from showing their guns. Slowly, Parker ambled his mount to where the brave stood. For a few moments, they conversed. The brave then eagerly accepted a stiff drink from the keg and scuttled into a strip of brush; they heard the thudding of hoofs soon afterwards. Parker chuckled, replaced the stopper of the cask and wheeled his horse.

'That is it,' he cheerfully informed the other men. 'The lookout is on his way to Tocho's camp to announce us. We can move on now.'

Vogel blinked. 'You are sure it is safe?'

'Relax, it is safe,' Parker assured him. 'Tocho knows my name.'

'Those lousy Injuns,' growled Ward, 'hate the guts of every white man.'

'But,' countered Parker, 'they would sell their souls for a bellyful of whiskey and that is what gives us the edge.' He jerked a thumb. 'Follow me.'

It took them another twenty-five minutes to locate the secret camp of the renegade Northern Paiute, so skillfully had the Indians camouflaged all approaches. The clearing was sizable and well-protected. The wigwams seemed to blend with the burnished brown and deep green of the tall trees in the background. From those wigwams, and from out of the timber to all sides of them, the braves appeared, converging on the six horsemen, brandishing muskets and staring with avid fascination at what Clay Parker, James Kruse and Frank Humes were carrying. Parker called for 'the great Chief Tocho, bravest of all the Northern Paiute,' and the most unprepossessing Indian ever encountered by the outlaws came trudging forward.

He was taller than the average Indian, of powerful physique and unusually ugly. His bare legs were bowed, the feet thrust into moccasins. His breech-clout and buckskin jacket were dirty. Any way you looked at him, Tocho was one mean Indian. He greeted Parker gruffly, curtly, and, during the muttered exchange that followed, the other white men sat their mounts, kept their faces impassive and their mouths shut – or just as Parker had told them to do.

Presently, Parker drawled an order to Kruse and Humes. 'Toss those kegs to the savages.'

'For Pete's sake, mind how you talk—' began Humes.

'Keep your shirt on, Frank.' Parker grinned. 'These Indian scoundrels don't understand a word of English. Go ahead. Give them the whiskey. Tocho's ready to talk a deal with me.'

All the men now dismounted. Two kegs were presented to Tocho's band, a dozen of whom immediately began a wild scuffle for possession of the fiery liquor. Parker removed the stopper of the third keg and offered it to Tocho. The chief of the renegades drank intensely and with such desperate enthusiasm that much of the raw whiskey slopped down the front of his buckskin jacket. He gulped, panting heavily. Then he spoke to Parker again, and Parker replied, coldly, decisively. It seemed Tocho hesitated, but only for a moment. He took another stiff pull at the whiskey. In the dialect of the Paiute, Parker slyly suggested, 'How much pleasure can there be for Tocho and his band in just this small quantity of firewater – when he could have more – much more?'

'This Maddox outfit and his freighters,' said Tocho, 'they have firewater in their wagons?'

'Perhaps,' shrugged Parker. 'But this is not important.'

'Because you have much firewater – and all of it for Tocho – if he will do as you ask?'

'That is my promise to you, Tocho. I want those wagons stopped. The men you will have to kill. The women and children, who knows? This is for you – the great Chief of the Paiute – to decide.' Parker was laying it on thick.

'All you ask,' said Tocho, 'is to search these wagons?'

Parker nodded. 'That is all I ask. We are too few to attack the men who drive the wagons but you, my brave friend, have many men under your command. It will be a great victory, and you will take many scalps – that I promise you.'

After another swig from the cask, the boss renegade's blood was up, his thirst uncontrollable; he was now Clay Parker's to command.

'We go now,' he breathed, his eyes agleam. 'You will take my brave warriors to this Maddox and his doomed friends and we will attack – and we will kill them all!' He whirled and began barking commands, and the camp seemed to come alive, to become a wild confusion of prancing horses and rifle toting braves dashing back and forth. But that confusion lasted only a few minutes. Soon, the renegades were mounted and ready to move. 'We go now!' Tocho stridently repeated.

At the gallop, nearly a hundred murderous braves followed Parker and his men out of the canyon and eastward, in the general direction of the route taken by the freighters. Many of those warriors had tasted the much-prized 'firewater' of the white man. The majority had not, but were eager to do so. They would stop at nothing to obtain a few mouthfuls of the liquor that irritated the senses and boosted their ego. They were like children demanding the fulfillment of a promise of candy except that they were a hundred times more dangerous, more lethal, than any child.

Hoofprints and wheel-ruts were discovered at a little after 9 o'clock, after which Parker gave the order to increase speed. In urgent haste, the attack force followed a seldom used trail through a forest of towering pines and onward, up and over a heavily forested ridge.

At ten o'clock, along the banks of a sluggish, almost dried-out creek, a halt was called to give the horses a break. During this wait, the casks were passed from hand to hand. Again, the chief of this band of renegade Indians drank intensely, and the cruelty was upon him. He forced himself to patience, but only because he realized the importance of not overtiring the horses. Track of the quarry was clear; Maddox's outfit had forded here.

'Due north – less than a half mile,' Parker quietly told his men, 'is one of the only wide open stretches in this part of Oregon. The Tabletop, it is called. It extends for about five miles and is all of two miles wide. I would say Maddox is bound to travel the Tabletop, because it is flat all the way, easy going for mule teams. Well, if we can overtake them anywhere on the Tabletop, they won't have a chance of survival. No cover. Not one rock to hide behind. In a running fight, they will be overtaken and cut down in the first quarter mile. Mules can move fast at times but not as fast as an Indian pony, and not when they are hauling heavily-laden wagons.'

'All right, Clay.' Humes beamed in eager anticipation. 'You want me to ride on ahead and scout?'

'Yeah, do that.' Parker nodded. 'But if you spot the wagons, make sure none of those mule skinners see you.'

'I will be back,' Frank Humes promised, 'by the time these bucks are ready to move again.'

And he was as good as his word. Tocho was about to order his warriors to remount, when Humes came pounding back to the north bank of the muddy creek.

'Was my hunch right?' Parker asked of his cohort.

'Yep, dead right,' declared Humes. 'They moved onto that plain a little while ago, and they ain't yet a quarter way across it.'

'Fantastic!' breathed Parker. 'It seems everything's going our way.'

He addressed Tocho in his own language, emphasizing that the terrain over which the quarry now moved offered ideal circumstances for a headlong attack. The chief of the renegades promptly relayed the news to his men, and the entire party began

127

putting distance between themselves and the muddy creek, moving northward at a good rate of speed. Discreetly, the six treacherous palefaces kept to the rear.

'No sense in getting within range of Maddox's gun,' was Parker's attitude. 'We will let Tocho handle the rough stuff and then we will move in quietly and help ourselves to the trunk and the loot.'

'After these red butchers have lifted their scalps,' sneered Levi Ward, 'and mutilated the dead, Consarn 'em – why do they do that?'

'We shouldn't begrudge them a little fun.' Parker snickered grimly. 'After all, they are gonna make us rich.'

'Clay, I never stood against you before,' called Ward, as they increased speed, 'but if the loot ain't in that damn trunk, if those women and kids die for no reason at all. . . .'

'It has to be in the Donahoe girl's trunk!' snapped Parker. 'There is no other explanation, no other place we haven't looked. And don't threaten me, Levi! I don't like to be threatened!'

At precisely 11:14 a.m., while Philip Mitchell was taking a turn at riding level with the lead wagon, and Maddox was handling the reins of the third team's mules, Mena Donahoe came forward and perched beside him on the driver's seat. This was the first really smooth stretch they had enjoyed, this steady run across the Tabletop. In the rear of the vehicle, cushioned by blankets, Myrtle Cross was actually able to nod off. Ahead in the second wagon, the eight children were joyfully singing. It was a lilting ditty that had been taught them by their prim but affectionate chaperone, Miss Bettie Erickson.

'I could not let this journey end,' Mena told Maddox, 'without explaining a few things to you—'

'Miss Donahoe,' he interrupted, 'we are many a long mile from this journey's end.'

'I am feeling a little guilty,' she whispered. 'That is why I have to talk to you, Mr Maddox. You have been so kind, so friendly. You treat me as though I were a real fine lady.'

'Well, doggone it,' he grinned, 'you ain't gonna complain, are you? And what is there to feel guilty about?'

'It is just' – she paused with a pained look on her face – 'that I don't think I am worthy of . . . of the way you seem to look up to me.'

'An old Maddox family habit, I'm afraid,' he cheerfully informed her. 'Maddox men were always taught to treat women with respect.'

'Maddox,' said Mena, 'you must have heard about what happened back in Battle Mountain, about how my father was murdered?'

'I heard about it,' he acknowledged. 'Didn't speak of it because I got no talent for offering sympathy. Speech making is somethin' I never learned.'

'He was a mighty likeable man – my father, I mean,' she sighed. 'I loved him, Mr Maddox, and did all I could do to help him, but I could never change the man he was. Nobody could reform Hugh Donahoe. He – he was a thief, Mr Maddox.' She was silent for a long moment, and so too was Glen Maddox. 'Did you ever hear of the Tulley gang?'

'Uh-huh, sure, who hasn't?' he said. 'Real bad medicine. Raised plenty of hell . . . what, many years ago. . . Been a while since I recall hearing much more about them.'

'That is because the gang was broken up,' she explained, 'after a bank robbery in a town called Sheep Springs—'

'I know of Sheep Springs,' he replied. 'Way down south, if I recall.'

'My father was captured and sent to prison – a five year stretch. They say he got away with all the money from that hold-up, that he managed to hide it before the law caught up with him. Well, maybe that is what really happened. Maybe it is the truth. I just don't know for sure. But one thing I suspect, Mr Maddox. I have the feeling he was killed by his old gang members. Not all of the Tulley gang were captured. There were five of them, maybe six, still on the loose while my dad was doing his time in prison.'

Maddox eyed her. 'And you think they got to him in Battle Mountain?'

'Men aren't murdered for no reason at all, Mr Maddox,' Mena shot back.

'Yeah, I reckon they aren't.'

'They all wanted the money. Dad claimed he didn't have it, but one of them – a man named Parker – went to see him in prison and tried to get my dad to tell him where the money is,' she explained.

'Miss Donahoe,' said Maddox, staring ahead, 'you don't have to tell me these things.'

'I thought you had a right to know the truth about me and my father,' she said in a loud voice.

'Speakin' of the truth,' he said with a frown, 'have you told all this to the feller that is about to have your hand in marriage?'

'All of it,' she assured him. 'I have no secrets from Antone.'

'That is how it ought to be.' He nodded approvingly. 'Everything fair and square, right from the start. Cards face up on the table.' Throwing her a sidelong grin, he added, 'It is how you deal with Antone that matters. How you deal with me – well – it ain't important at all. I am just a mule freighter that is shippin' you from one place to another, and you don't owe me any explanations about anything.'

'Can the daughter of an ex-convict,' she wistfully wondered, 'call herself a lady?'

'I will bust the jaw,' grinned Maddox, 'of any fool that says you ain't.'

'You do remind me of Antone,' she declared. 'Just as kindly – just as understanding. . . .' She stopped talking abruptly and became tense, and he felt her hand gripping his arm. When next she spoke, her voice was high-pitched, edgy. 'What – what was that?'

Maddox had already heard the sound too, and had recognized it for what it was. The guarantee of trouble. The threat of violent death. War cries! The shrill yipping of Indians moving to attack. He glanced hurriedly over his shoulder and gave vent to

131

a vehement oath.

So many of them!

They were appearing just over the slight elevation – this body of Indians – damn near a hundred, coming on fast.

This caught Maddox by surprise at first, as Indians were often seen on the plains. He soon figured out, however, that they were on no friendly errand, and he believed them to be a raiding party of the Paiute tribe. They were decked in their war paint, and as soon as they saw Maddox look their way, raised a shout.

What in the hell had happened to the peace treaty signed by the Paiute? These were definitely Paiute – Northern Paiute, Maddox surmised – nothing surer. Even at a distance, tutored by an expert. Galen Maddox had been a scout for the army, before becoming a freighter. From his father, young Glen had learned a great deal of the ways of the Indians and could speak fluently in several dialects.

His companions, fearing that they were in the presence of an enemy who would doubtless endeavor to relieve them of their lives, made signals to Maddox that they too had seen the imminent attack. He used plain and graphic English when he bellowed orders to his men.

'Get those mules runnin' fast! Have your hardware handy for when these crazy bucks catch up with us because they sure will catch up with us! When they get in range, stall your rigs, get behind 'em and start shootin'! You women and kids all need to stay low!'

Maddox tried a few friendly signals towards the advancing Indians, however, those signals were ignored. The Indians continued to advance on the wagons.

From the first wagon, Liam Buford bellowed an offer. 'If anybody can loan us a couple rifles, Wayne and I will handle our share of the fighting!'

The howling braves were drawing closer. Like well-trained cavalry, they fanned out then gradually moved to get on both sides of the wagons. This was a common Indian mode of attack. They began to fire then.

'Back!' barked Maddox.

And, with a sudden sweeping motion of his arm, he sent the startled Mena pitching backward off the driver's seat to fall beside the prone Myrtle Cross, who promptly grabbed at her and pressed her face to the wagon bed.

To operate the reins for four spans of hard running mules one-handed was no easy chore, but Maddox managed it. He emptied his holster, as Philip and Jacob, straddling the two saddlers, increased speed and began riding level with the second rig.

The Indians were riding closer and firing at them. Maddox returned fire as did most of his freighters over the backs of the mules and horses. They continued to get closer, when a shot from the gun of one of the freighters killed an Indian. A rush now was made upon them. A musket ball screamed past Maddox's head. Another struck Jacob, who pitched in his saddle, but somehow he managed to remain mounted. Maddox cursed luridly, thumbed back his hammer and half-turned on the seat. A yelling Indian, cutting loose with his musket, was coming up fast on the wagon's right side. Raising his Colt, narrowing his eyes along its barrel for only a short moment, Maddox squeezed the trigger. The young buck quit shouting and plunged backwards from his fast moving pony.

From the seat of the second rig, Ellis Allum opened fire with a Winchester, leaving the driving to Claus Becker. From the seat of the lead wagon, Uncle Jack Munson whipped his team to their utmost effort and the tobacco chewing Texas John Quayle began wreaking havoc with a shotgun. But such a running fight could not be prolonged because, already, the mules were tiring.

CHAPTER 10

MADDOX DELIVERS

They were more than halfway across the vast plain, when Glen Maddox gave the order to halt and make a stand. The Indians formed a circle around them. The circle was contracted while the freighters kept up their fire.

The animals ridden by the attacking Northern Paiute showed no sign of tiring, while the hard-pressed mules were faltering. To either side of the lumbering wagons, the mounted Indians were closing in. The empty rifles of the freighters had been discarded in favor of six-shooters. At almost point-blank range, Maddox triggered at another screaming brave, sending him backwards off his pony in a somersault.

'Stall 'em here! Form a triangle! Uncle Jack, point your team west! Claus, you aim your leaders at the rear of the first wagon and do it fast!' Maddox screamed.

He hauled back on his reins and, in that unpredictable, seemingly pointless way so typical of the Indians, the Northern Paiute withdrew slightly, falling back as though to permit the freighters to form their triangle, the better to prolong the battle. Jacob Maher was clinging to his saddle horn, his torso bloody, his face ashen. Wayne Buford was huddled on the bed of the lead wagon, unconscious from loss of blood; a musket ball had lodged in the fleshy part of his right left shoulder. Both Uncle Jack and Ellis Allum were wounded, but only superficially – thus far. As near as Maddox could judge, the women and children were still unscathed.

Ellis waited for Uncle Jack to turn the lead team, then nudged his own animals towards the tailgate of the first rig and jerked them to a halt. Simultaneously, Maddox swung his team leftward and forward, so that his leaders were stalled but a few feet from Uncle Jack's, and the right corner of his end wagon almost touched the left corner of that driven by Ellis – and the triangle was formed.

Glen Maddox threw a glance to his rear, and to right and left. The Indians were bunching up to begin a charge. Plague take these crazy Paiutes! Weren't they supposed to have signed a treaty?

'What do you make of 'em, Maddox?' called Texas John.

'Paiute – Northern Paiute for sure,' growled Maddox. 'Renegades is my best guess; a passel of bucks that flew the coop – quit the reservation.'

'Some passel,' snapped Ellis. 'Must be nigh on a hunnerd of 'em out there.'

'Well, damn and blast their ornery innards,' mumbled Philip. 'We been whittlin' 'em down a bit.'

'Everybody get reloaded,' ordered Maddox. 'Miss Mena, Mrs Cross – you head on over to the second rig and lend Miss Bettie a hand, and tell her I said to keep those young'uns out of sight, heads down.' He dropped to the ground, ejected his spent shells and dug fresh cartridges from his belt. 'Ellis! Help Philip off his horse and stash him in the front wagon. Tell Uncle Jack to tend to him as best as he can. Anybody that ain't hurt too bad to use a gun, c'mon over here to me.'

By the time his Colt was reloaded, they were joining him – Texas John, Claus, Philip and Ellis – the latter striving to ignore the agony of a bullet gashed leg. The second last to arrive was Liam Buford, grim-faced and hefting a shotgun. The last, to the wonderment of all, was Mena Donahoe. As she crouched beside him, by a rear wheel of the third wagon, she vehemently asserted, 'Somebody has to loan me a gun! I have to help because I keep thinking of those poor kids and Bettie. . . .'

'Get back to that damn-blasted wagon!' raged Maddox.

'There isn't time,' she retorted. 'Somebody had better give me a gun in a hurry. Here they come again!'

The Indians were charging. They rendered themselves a constantly shifting target, shifting from side to side on their ponies.

'Here,' grunted Ellis, as he passed her his Colt and readied his Winchester.

'Well,' said Liam Buford, 'I guess – uh – this is it.'

'I would like to know,' scowled Maddox, 'what got these savage bucks so fired up.'

The circle the Northern Paiute had formed gradually became smaller in diameter, when a shot from the gun of Claus Becker killed one of the charging braves. A second rush was now made upon them.

The charge was in full swing. Filling the air with strident, blood-curdling yells, the Paiute came pounding towards the stalled wagons from a distance of well over a hundred yards, but were now closer. The freighters traded sober glances. Claus spat from the corner of his mouth and remarked, 'Sure is a herd of 'em, ain't there? I always did say Injuns must breed like jack rabbits.'

And then, suddenly, the idea was born in Maddox's mind. Far-fetched? Futile? Childish, maybe? No. Not when applied to the psychology of the Northern Paiute. Even blood-thirsty savages had their own peculiar code. If he could reach the leader of this bunch – bamboozle him into a man-to-man showdown.

'Hold your fire,' he quietly ordered his men.

'You crazy or somethin'?' challenged Philip Mitchell. 'They will be on top of us pretty soon!'

'There is a trick I aim to try,' muttered Maddox. 'If it don't work – well – we will just have to get to shootin'. But if I can faze their chief, force him out

138

into the open, there is an even chance we will get out of this hassle and keep our scalps.'

As he began rising, Texas John bitterly announced, 'There is a bunch of whites in back of them Injuns. Ah just now spotted 'em – about five or six it looks like.'

'I would say that is very interesting,' growled Maddox, 'plumb interesting indeed.'

And now, ignoring their protests and Mena's startled scream, he clambered up the sideboard of the wagon to the top of its canvas canopy, rising into clear view of the advancing riders. The clatter of hoofs was loud, but so was the voice of Glen Maddox, strengthened by years of full-throated yelling at recalcitrant mules. Also, he was using the language of the Paiute tribe, which came as somewhat of a surprise to them. But, most important of all, he wasn't yelling for mercy, suing for peace, begging for a parley. He was bellowing abuse, roaring scathing insults.

'Your chief is a woman – a weak-bellied, spineless woman, a coward and a fool! Who leads the Paiute today? I dare him to face me!'

Liam Buford clamped a hand to Mena's trembling shoulder and muttered, 'I wouldn't have believed it possible. Look, Miss Mena! They hesitate!'

And hesitate they did. Already a score of war-painted bucks had reined up, the better to catch the gist of Maddox's tirade. The others were still advancing, but at a slower rate. One rider – Tocho – was urging them on. They heard him, but they also heard Maddox.

'Who leads this band of Paiute to certain death? I dare him to name himself!'

The chief of the renegades, Tocho, jerked his pony to a halt, glared wildly to his right and left and to his rear. His men were hanging back, waiting. As their chief, it was his prerogative to meet every challenge; the leader of the Northern Paiute war party had to be the mightiest warrior of all – such was the tradition.

He gesticulated angrily, yelled a reply, 'I lead the Paiute this day! I, Tocho!'

'Tocho?' jeered Maddox. 'I will skin the scalp from this Tocho! He is a coward and a fool, unworthy to lead brave warriors into battle!'

'Tocho knows no fear!' the chief of the renegades vehemently retorted.

'So few palefaces – and so many of you,' countered Maddox. 'Only a coward would attack so few, with so many braves to support him!' He clambered down from atop the wagon, crawled under it and stepped out into plain view of the bunched war party, while his friends held their breath.

Tocho sat his stamping pinto less than fifty yards away.

Deliberately, Maddox unbuckled and discarded his gun belt. 'I offer you a bargain, Tocho. . . .' He was still raising his voice, making sure every word carried to Tocho's band of braves. 'You have seen our women. . . .'

'Your women,' bragged Tocho, 'will be *my* women!'

'If you can kill me!' yelled Maddox. 'If you have the courage to fight me! There will be only the two of us, Tocho!' He had peeled off his jacket and was unfastening his shirt. 'One against one! Use a knife, brave warrior! I will meet you unarmed! No gun. No knife. No weapon of any kind. Only my bare hands!'

Tocho cast another glance to his rear. The braves were eyeing him unblinkingly, awaiting his reaction. Only too well, he realized the inevitable penalties of his dodging this challenge. He would have to fight his bull-voiced paleface.

Maddox tossed his shirt aside, removed his hat. Bare to the waist, he took four steps forward.

'All may witness!' he called out. 'My men will not fire on this band of Paiute!'

'What is your bargain?' barked the renegade chief.

'If you can kill me,' boomed Maddox, 'my men will surrender!'

'What is Maddox saying to him?' Liam Buford demanded anxiously.

'Don't you fret yourself, mister,' Claus Becker drawled assuredly, 'Maddox knows what he's doin'.'

'If you are defeated,' Maddox finished, 'your braves must retreat, and leave us in peace. A coward would not accept such terms, Tocho!'

'Tocho is no coward!' gasped the renegade chief, hastily dismounting. 'I am the bravest warrior!'

'Then prove it!' Maddox curtly invited, after which he called to his fellow freighters in English, briefly explaining his intentions.

The pinto pranced clear. The Northern Paiute

band advanced a little closer, but to watch, not to brandish or discharge their muskets at the small knot of people on the other side of the third wagon. Tocho had discarded his headdress. A large knife about the size of a Bowie gleamed wickedly in his right hand, as he darted towards his paleface challenger.

'He can't hope to win!' fretted Liam Buford. 'He is at a tremendous disadvantage!'

'That is for sure, Mr Buford, suh,' agreed Texas John. 'That is for dang sure.'

'And you don't care?' demanded the would-be newspaper man.

'Me?' The Texan blinked. 'Care what happens to one lousy Injun? Not much, Mr Buford. Not this man.'

'I mean Maddox, your boss!' gasped Buford. 'He is at a disadvantage! The Indian has a knife, Mr Maddox is unarmed.'

'Friend,' grinned Claus, while Texas John began to chuckle softly, 'that knife don't mean a durn thing to a scrapper as salty as Glen Maddox. Wouldn't matter if that Paiute chief was chargin' at him with a lance even, or a bayonet. That Injun is as good as whupped already. You just watch – see how Maddox pulls his doggone feathers.'

Far back to the rear of the bunched Paiute band, Clay Parker and his gang of outlaws were in somewhat of a quandary. James Kruse demanded to know what was happening, and Parker sourly replied, 'I would tell you if I knew. I haven't quite figured that out yet. All I know is we aren't budging.'

Teeth bared in a leer of savage anticipation, Tocho leapt. The point of his blade darted forward, then swept upward. That first thrust barely penetrated Maddox's skin, because he nimbly back stepped and, because he arched his back, the up-thrust missed his chin by a full three inches. Tocho barged in close and tried again, a wild, vicious slash aimed at Maddox's throat. Maddox ducked low, actually dropped to one knee in the process, so that the lethal blade swung clear over his bent back – he felt the whoosh of air through his hair – and now he was ready to retaliate.

His bunched right hand hurled forward, slamming into Tocho's belly with devastating force, propelled by every ounce of his considerable muscle power. The renegade chief grunted, groaned and began sagging. Maddox seized the opportunity to grab for the knife, but missed unfortunately. His adversary rallied faster than he anticipated. The point of the blade loomed before his face, sunlight shined in Maddox's eyes. Maddox was able to sidestep the blade and threw a jolting left fist to Tocho's face; he followed it with a powerful uppercut that sent the Northern Paiute stumbling backward for about five yards or so. Then, when Tocho halted and began raising the knife once more, Maddox leapt at him like a blood-crazed mountain lion, firmly grasping the Indian's right wrist to prevent him lunging with the knife, using his own bunched right to drive punishing blows to the face and belly of the renegade chief. Tocho grappled with him and the two men went to the ground in a tangled, threshing heap, but with Maddox still maintaining his grip. Again and again, he struck with his bunched right fist. He mangled the renegade's ear, closed an eye, bruised almost every inch of the swarthy face. Then, for a finale, he straddled his victim, pinning him to the ground. Tocho, gasping for breath, felt the knife whisked from his grip, felt the point of it prodding his throat. His eyes dilated.

In fluent and compelling Paiute patois, Glen Maddox offered another bargain.

'I might spare your life, Tocho.'

'You have . . . already won,' groaned the renegade chief. 'My warriors will honor this bargain. Your people will be left in peace . . . after you kill me. . . .'

'Life is sweet,' Maddox pointed out.

'Yes . . . life is sweet,' Tocho fervently agreed.

'I see white men far behind your warriors,' frowned Maddox. 'Answer my questions, Tocho. Speak straight and true and I will spare your life.'

Sullen, Tocho replied, 'I will answer.'

'You smell of the white man's firewater – the whiskey. Is that how they persuaded you to attack us?'

'Yes. Much firewater was promised to me and my band....'

'Who are these men?' demanded Maddox.

'One is called Parker, another Gobson. I do not know the names of all of them. . . .'

'That is all you know? They did not say why my people should be attacked?' pressed Maddox.

'The paleface called Parker said kill all but no

burning. No fire-arrows.' Tocho was struggling to breath.

The Northern Paiute warriors exhaled noisily, as Maddox drew the point of the blade away from the throat of their chief. Roughly, Maddox hauled him to his feet. He then raised the knife for the lynx-eyed warriors to see and, with a quick, deft movement, lowered it and returned it to the sheath at Tocho's waist.

'Now,' he said, standing very close to the sore and sorry renegade chief. 'Remember that I understand your tongue. Let me hear you give the order for all the Paiute warriors and braves to depart this place.'

'They were promised firewater,' mumbled Tocho.

'Come with me,' growled Maddox. He grasped the renegade's arm, walked him a few yards closer to the wagons and shouted a command, 'Hey, Uncle Jack! Show yourself!'

With a rifle tucked under his arm, the aged cook limped into clear view of Tocho and the bunched Northern Paiute. Maddox indicated Uncle Jack with a dramatic gesture and launched into a short and vehement speech, still in the language of the Indians. When he had finished, the braves began moving away. All appeared impressed and not a little frightened. Tocho's eyes were dilated again.

'Now go,' Maddox told him. 'Take your warriors, collect your dead and wounded, then go back to the reservation. Stay away from the paleface called Parker.'

He was re-donning his clothes by the time the

145

Northern Paiute were galloping southward across the Tabletop, and he was ignoring the cries of relief raised by the women and children, the fervent compliments aimed at him by his men. Right now, Maddox was mainly concerned with the six riders in the background. He called a query to Mena, as he strapped on his gun belt around his waist.

'You ever hear your father speak of a man the name of Parker and another named Gobson?'

'Yes.' She nodded. 'Parker, Gobson, Ward and some others. All of them rode with the Tulley gang in the old days.'

'What are you gettin' at, Maddox?' demanded Texas John.

'Those six skunks headin' for the yonder,' scowled Maddox, 'bribed those crazy warriors with whiskey – put 'em up to raidin' us. Claus, my boy, I will be obliged if you will fetch the bay and the sorrel. I aim to have me a showdown with those polecats.'

'Why, in heaven's name,' wondered Liam Buford, 'would white men bribe savages to—'

'They wanted something we are totin',' stated Maddox, looking directly at Mena.

'Too bad we only got a couple horses,' lamented Texas John, as he armed himself with a Winchester. 'Still, a couple of us oughta be plenty. After all, Maddox, there is only a half dozen of 'em.'

'If you think you can leave me out of this hassle,' grinned Claus Becker, 'you got another think comin'. Me and you's ridin' double on the sorrel, Johnny.'

Somebody tossed a Winchester to Maddox. He caught it, strode over to the bay gelding and swung astride. Over his shoulder, as he hustled the animal away from the wagons, he called a warning to his man, Philip Mitchell.

'Stay put and keep your eyes peeled, just in case those Injuns came sneakin' back.'

CHAPTER 11

OUTLAWS VS. FREIGHTERS

Texas John and Claus Becker, both hefting Winchesters, were double-loaded on the sorrel which nevertheless hit a fine tune of speed, galloping after the racing bay that toted Maddox. The quarry, six very disgruntled outlaws, were clearly visible and moving as fast as their horses could carry them.

A good distance separated them from their pursuers; this might have become a lengthy chase had Clay Parker not glanced backward and observed.

'Only two horses and three men at the most! We outnumber them, so why should we run?' He barked a command to his fellow outlaws. 'Slow down. This is as far as we go until we have to attend to these wannabe heroes.'

As they reined their horses up, Peter Vogel sourly

148

questioned Parker. 'What about the money?'

'First things first, Vogel,' snapped a tense Clay Parker. 'We have to take care of this Maddox fellow and his freighters. Time enough later for figuring some new strategy for getting the money.' He wheeled his mount, emptied his holster and frowned towards the approaching riders. 'Only three of them, boys. Two on a sorrel. One on the bay. This is going to be plumb easy picking. Spread out, boys, and pick them off as soon as they get within range. We need to make short work of them.'

Vogel and Carl Gobson had already dismounted their horses and were readying rifles. To hunt cover would have been superfluous; and they were still on the Tabletop. Grim-faced, Levi Ward, James Kruse and Frank Humes cocked their six-gun and followed the approach of the hard-ridden bay and the panting sorrel. And then, abruptly, the pursuers halted their mounts and leapt to the ground.

'What the hell are they doin'?' gasped Gobson. 'They are too far way to score on us, even with those rifles!'

'Hush!' snapped Parker, waving his hand at Gobson and the others. He shared the same concerns.

From a distance that might have discouraged lesser marksmen, Glen Maddox, Texas John and Claus Becker cut loose with their Winchesters and gave the lie to Gobson's assertion. They had made all due allowances for the distance and their calculations had been deadly accurate. A .44-40 slug knocked Carl

Gobson sprawling before he could draw a bead on any of the three. Another lodged in Levi Ward's gun arm, just above the elbow. He gave vent to an anguished groan and toppled from his mount. Parker and the others began shooting return fire fast, only now did they realize that they – not the freighters – were at a disadvantage. Maddox, Claus and the Texan were sprawled flat on their bellies, thus presenting very small targets for their adversaries.

Across the Tabletop, the barking of rifles mingled with the booming of six guns and, too late, James Kruse began dismounting to go to the ground. Just as his feet struck earth, a well-aimed slug from the barking rifle of Glen Maddox slammed into his chest with a sickening thud. He died with a curse on his lips, lurching back against his startled horse and then collapsing in an untidy heap.

One by one, the freighters discarded their rifles, rose up, drew their pistols and ran hard towards the surviving outlaws. Their rifles were empty but, as soon as they came close enough, they would wreak havoc with their pistols. Frantically, Vogel resumed shooting, aiming quickly, triggering in urgent haste, while Parker and Humes helped themselves to the weapons dropped by Ward and Kruse. With a pistol in each hand, they crouched and cut loose at the oncoming trio of attackers. One of Vogel's wildly triggered slugs creased Maddox's ribs. He stumbled, fell, lurched to his feet and returned fire, and Peter Vogel died whining. Claus spun drunkenly, shoved off-balance by the impact of a bullet gashing his left shoulder. From a kneeling poster, he coolly drew a bead and fired at Humes. His shot missed. Then, just as Humes took aim at him, Texas John stepped in front of Claus, shielding him and fanning three shots in rapid succession, two of which mortally wounded Frank Humes and sent him hurtling to the ground.

Clay Parker's scalp crawled. His own pistol, and the weapon taken from the wounded Levi Ward, still contained several live cartridges. He was within leaping distance of a horse and Maddox was on his feet again, stumbling towards Parker, snarling oaths and demanding his surrender.

'Give it up!'

For just a second, Parker hesitated. Then, whirling around, he lined both pistols on the oncoming Glen Maddox.

'Watch out!' yelled Texas John.

'He's mine!' roared Maddox, simultaneous with the booming of his own pistol.

Jolted by the impact of the bullet, Parker gritted his teeth and discharged his right-hand weapon. But, by then, he was losing strength, his hand had sagged, and the bullet hit ground a full five feet in front of Maddox. He groaned an oath, struggled to lift his gun-filled left hand, but never quite made it. His eyes glazed over and, with his shirtfront showing a nasty blotch of red, he crumpled and fell.

The grim silence that followed was broken only by the anguished groans of Levi

Ward, Maddox, Claus and Texas John were all wounded, but were not the groaning type. While the

Texas explored the saddle bags of the outlaws, found a bottle and fed a stiff shot to Claus, Maddox did the same for the distraught Ward. The outlaw gulped gratefully and begged for a doctor, insisting that the pain of his injured arm was well-nigh unbearable.

'You will have to settle for mule skinners' doctorin',' growled Maddox. 'Our cook'll dig that slug out of you and, if your luck holds, you might still be alive when we turn you over to the law in the next town we come to.' He added, 'Mind now, that depends on whether you aim to answer my questions. You play dumb, for instance, and we'll leave you here for the buzzards to come pickin' at you.'

'And we ain't foolin',' drawled Texas John.

'Hell, no,' grunted Claus. 'We sure don't owe you no favors – after you bribin' them Injuns to lift our scalps.'

'That wasn't my idea,' panted Ward. 'Aw, what's the use? I am jailbait, anyway. Ask me anything, and you'll get answers. You want to know why Parker set you up for a massacre? It's because of the Donahoe girl. Parker figures she is totin' all the loot from the old Sheep Springs hold-up five years ago. . . .'

He went on to describe the whole shoddy conspiracy devised by the unscrupulous Clay Parker, including Parker's butchering of Mena's father in a fit of insane rage and his subsequent decision to have the entire Maddox outfit wiped out by Tocho's band of Paiute, and all for the sake of whatever might be concealed in Mena Donahoe's trunk.

'That is all of it,' he gasped, at the end. 'And now

. . . I don't much care . . . what happens next.'

Those were his last words for some little time. Nauseated by loss of blood, he lapsed into unconsciousness. Maddox and his freighters had also done their share of bleeding, but weren't about to faint. They used whiskey as a makeshift antiseptic for their wounds, as well as a temporary booster for the pain and their strength, before gathering the dead outlaws and draping them across their horses. There would be a burial party on the Tabletop this day, but not until the injuries suffered by the freighters had received such treatment as could be offered by Uncle Jack.

CHAPTER 12

THE JOURNEY CONTINUES AND ENDS

It was mid-afternoon before the journey north was resumed. Five unmarked graves were left at the freighters' campsite, and the spare horses were tethered to the tailgates of the big freight wagons. The injuries of Maddox and his two companions had been treated and, in time, would heal. Mercifully, the women and children had emerged unscathed from the whole ordeal, a fact for which Maddox was humbly grateful. He could stand unlimited pain, but didn't relish the sight of a child bleeding from a scraped knee, let alone dying from a mortal wound.

Again, he chose to travel in the third wagon, with

Mena sharing the driver's seat. He repeated every detail of the confession pulled from the now bandaged and helpless Levi Ward, and her reaction convinced him that she was innocent of any complicity in her father's larcenous activities.

'I guess it is possible that Dad stashed the money before his arrest,' she mused, 'and he might have had time to retrieve it after his discharge from Fort Shelborne. But I don't know, Mr Maddox. . . .'

'He wasn't very bright, your father,' Maddox said.

'Oh, he was smart,' she warmly assured him. 'Too smart for his own good – never at a loss for some new and far-fetched notion, some get rich soon scheme. . . .'

'All right,' said Maddox. 'If he was all that smart, maybe he did figure a way to plant that money in your trunk.'

'I promise you,' said Mena, 'when we make night camp, I'll check every inch of that trunk, and ask Mrs Cross to help me. If I'm carrying that money, Mr Maddox, I just don't know it.'

'If you find it . . .' he began.

'If I find it,' she finished, 'you may be sure I'll turn it over to the sheriff of the first town we come to.'

'That will be Cordero Springs,' he told her. 'We ought to reach Cordero Springs around midday tomorrow and Stag Ridge the day after.'

Their night camp was the grassy floor of a rock-walled box canyon, sheltered from the elements, made cheerful by the glow of the large fire prepared by Uncle Jack and Jacob Maher. The evening meal

155

was prepared and eaten, after a fervent grace offered by the still-shaken Bettie Erickson. And, during the meal, all the children were paraded before Maddox and his hard-bitten freighters to solemnly repeat the speech of gratitude taught to them by their chaperone. Rough though they were, the freighters were deeply touched.

By lamplight, and with assistance from Myrtle Cross, Mena investigated every article, every item of clothing in her trunk, checked the inside of the lid and every inch of the cloth lining, but without locating any trace of a high-denomination banknote. And then, after the trunk had been repacked, the inspiration smote her with all the impact of a physical blow. Why hadn't she thought of it before?

'Is it normal,' she wondered, 'for a father to give his daughter a corset . . . for a wedding gift?'

'Normal?' Myrtle snorted in keen disapproval. 'Hardly.'

'He insisted I should never part with it,' said Mena. 'What's more, he had it made specially, back in White Pines.'

'By a seamstress naturally?' Myrtle presumed.

'That seamstress was an old and trusted friend,' Mena recalled, clasping her hands to her trim waist. 'Will you help me, please? If you'll fetch the lantern and a pair of scissors, we'll go off into the rocks and I'll take off Dad's wedding gift. When we start cutting into that silk, we might just find. . . .'

'Seventy-five thousand dollars?' gasped Myrtle. 'Surely not!'

Fifteen minutes later, within the concealment of a rock cleft some short distance from the camp, Mena was readjusting her clothing and following the older woman's movements with intense interest. Very carefully, Myrtle slit the outer silk of that intimate undergarment. One end of a sliver of whalebone immediately protruded. Myrtle pulled it out and, from the slot thus revealed, there spilled several tiny balls of paper – green coloured paper.

'Don't let the wind blow them away!' cautioned Mena.

Myrtle gathered the tiny balled pieces of paper into her left palm and began unrolling one. Wrinkled and aged it was, and none too clean, but negotiable – very negotiable.

'Land's sakes and heavens to Betsey!' breathed Myrtle. 'A thousand dollar bill!'

In the settlement of Cordero Springs, ten minutes after noon of the following day, the wounded Levi Ward was handed into the custody of the local sheriff, as was also a neat package containing $75,000, the money from the Sheep Springs Community Bank robbery from five years prior.

Mena Donahoe was glad to be rid of it; the Cordero Springs authorities could be relied upon to ensure its return to the banking company from whence it had come.

At Deerhorn Pass, the next day, Mena and her baggage were unloaded, and Glen Maddox personally handed her into the care of her tall and good-looking fiancé, who humbly thanked the freighters for delivering his bride safe and unharmed.

That same day, in the late afternoon, Bettie Erickson and her small charges were delivered to the eagerly awaiting nesters and their wives in the town square of Pattonville, the small town in the heart of Laurel Valley. The freighters didn't linger here, because the gratitude of the locals and the adulation of the children was, as Texas John, put it, 'Plumb discomfortin'.'

And they had another reason for coaxing the utmost speed out of their teams. Myrtle Cross was still determined to reach her destination in time for the birth of her first grandchild. She arranged for the dispatching of a telegraph message from Pattonville, climbed back into the third rig and demanded that Maddox give the order to depart immediately.

Mid-morning the following day, when the heavy rigs lumbered to a halt in her daughter's town, Myrtle was greeted by a self-conscious young man with flaming red hair, solemn green eyes and a hesitant way of speaking. After he had nervously kissed her cheek, Myrtle surveyed him haughtily and said, 'Come now, son-in-law, take me to my daughter. Now that I've arrived, we can proceed with all the necessary arrangements. I presume you've already consulted a qualified physician? Well? Don't just stand there blinking. Say something!'

'Mother Cross,' frowned her son-in-law, 'didn't you ever have the notion that young'un might be born before you got here?'

'The nerve of that child! It wouldn't dare!' boomed Myrtle. 'And neither would my daughter!'

'Well. . .' The young man blinked at the impassive mule skinners, fidgeted uncomfortably. 'I guess we all three of us owe you an apology, Mother Cross. I mean . . . your daughter and me – and the little one. . . .'

'No!' gasped Myrtle.

'He has arrived,' confessed the uneasy father, 'three days ago, in fact.'

The freighters did not linger; the wrath of Myrtle Cross compelled them to be on their way. Two days later, the Buford brothers were disembarked in the bustling Oregon township of Klamath Falls and, while the freighters were beginning their return journey to the south, the printing press was already being unpacked and assembled. Soon, despite his shoulder wound, Wayne Buford would begin production of the *Klamath Falls Observer*'s first issue.

It wasn't until they were three hours south of Klamath Falls that the oldest member of the outfit thought to ask Maddox, 'Just what in tarnation did you tell them lousy Injuns about me, back when you whupped their chief?'

'Oh yeah, that.' Maddox shrugged nonchalantly. 'Well, don't you worry about it, Uncle Jack.'

'I ain't worryin',' replied Uncle Jack. 'I'm only askin' out of curiosity.'

'If I tell you what I told Tocho and his warriors, you have to promise not to get mad.' Maddox grinned.

'Why would I get mad?' demanded a puzzled Uncle Jack.

'Well,' said Maddox, 'it's thisaway. Those Paiute braves had been leanin' on the rye real heavy, you see, gettin' stewed to the ears on firewater – whiskey, you know what I mean? I figured this'd be a chance to scare 'em off liquor for their whole lives.'

'So?' prodded Uncle Jack.

'So,' said Maddox, 'I told them you had been drinkin' whiskey since you were fifteen years old and look what it had done to you. I told them how it made you old before your time. Matter of fact, I told 'em you were only twenty-four years old and they believed it.'

'You got your doggone nerve, Glen Maddox.' The old man scowled at Maddox.

'A freighter has to have nerve,' countered Maddox, with well-timed diplomacy. 'And I had a couple of good teachers, my dad and you – Uncle Jack.'

'Well . . .' shrugged Uncle Jack, 'when you put it thataway. . . .'

'And now what, Mad-dox?' called Texas John.

'And now,' replied Maddox, 'we head south and find us another cargo. That is what we freighters do.'